Praise for Debbie Macomber's bestselling novels
from Ballantine Books

Must Love Flowers

"A testament to the power of new beginnings. Wise, warm, witty, and charmingly full of hope, this story celebrates the surprising and unexpected ways that family, friendship, and love can lift us up."
—KRISTIN HANNAH,
bestselling author of *The Nightingale*

"Uplifting, warm, and hopeful. With her signature charm and wit, Debbie Macomber proves that the best relationships, like the perfect blooms, are always worth the wait. . . . This can't-miss novel is Macomber at the height of her storytelling prowess. I absolutely adored it!"
—KRISTY WOODSON HARVEY, *New York Times*
bestselling author of *The Summer of Songbirds*

"Debbie Macomber never fails to deliver an uplifting, heart-warming story. Whether you're just starting out, just starting over, or anything in between, *Must Love Flowers* should be at the top of your summer reading list!"
—BRENDA NOVAK, *New York Times*
bestselling author of *Before We Were Strangers*

The Best Is Yet to Come

"Macomber's latest is a wonderful inspirational read that has just enough romance as the characters heal their painful emotional wounds." —*Library Journal*

"This tale of redemption and kindness is a gift to Macomber's many readers and all who love tales of sweet and healing romance." —*Booklist*

Cottage by the Sea

"Romantic, warm, and a breeze to read—one of [Debbie] Macomber's best." —*Kirkus Reviews*

"Macomber never disappoints. Tears and laughter abound in this story of loss and healing that will wrap you up and pull you in; readers will finish it in one sitting."
—*Library Journal* (starred review)

"Macomber's story of tragedy and triumph is emotionally engaging from the outset and ends with a satisfying conclusion. Readers will be most taken by the characters, particularly Annie, a heartwarming lead who bolsters the novel."
—*Publishers Weekly*

Any Dream Will Do

"*Any Dream Will Do* is . . . so realistic, it's hard to believe it's fiction through the end. Even then, it's hard to say goodbye to these characters. This standalone novel will make you hope it becomes a Hallmark movie, or gets a sequel. It's an inspiring, hard-to-put-down tale. . . . You need to read it."
—*The Free Lance–Star*

"*Any Dream Will Do* by Debbie Macomber is a study in human tolerance and friendship. Macomber masterfully shows how all people have value." —*Fresh Fiction*

If Not for You

"A heartwarming story of forgiveness and unexpected love."
—*Harlequin Junkie*

"A fun, sweet read." —*Publishers Weekly*

A Girl's Guide to Moving On

"Beloved author Debbie Macomber reaches new heights in this wise and beautiful novel. It's the kind of reading experience that comes along only rarely, bearing the hallmarks of a classic. The timeless wisdom in these pages will stay with you long after the book is closed."
—SUSAN WIGGS, #1 *New York Times*
bestselling author of *Starlight on Willow Lake*

"Debbie dazzles! A wonderful story of friendship, forgiveness, and the power of love. I devoured every page!"
—SUSAN MALLERY, #1 *New York Times* bestselling
author of *The Friends We Keep*

Last One Home

"Fans of bestselling author Macomber will not be disappointed by this compelling stand-alone novel." —*Library Journal*

ROSE HARBOR

Sweet Tomorrows

"Macomber fans will leave the Rose Harbor Inn with warm memories of healing, hope, and enduring love."
—*Kirkus Reviews*

"Overflowing with the poignancy, sweetness, conflicts and romance for which Debbie Macomber is famous, *Sweet Tomorrows* captivates from beginning to end." —*Bookreporter*

"Fans will enjoy this final installment of the Rose Harbor series as they see Jo Marie's story finally come to an end."
—*Library Journal*

Silver Linings

"Macomber's homespun storytelling style makes reading an easy venture. . . . She also tosses in some hidden twists and turns that will delight her many longtime fans." —*Bookreporter*

"Reading Macomber's novels is like being with good friends, talking and sharing joys and sorrows."
—*New York Journal of Books*

Love Letters

"[Debbie] Macomber's mastery of women's fiction is evident in her latest. . . . [She] breathes life into each plotline, carefully intertwining her characters' stories to ensure that none of them overshadow the others. Yet it is her ability to capture different facets of emotion which will entrance fans and newcomers alike." —*Publishers Weekly*

"Romance and a little mystery abound in this third installment of Macomber's series set at Cedar Cove's Rose Harbor Inn. . . . Readers of Robyn Carr and Sherryl Woods will enjoy Macomber's latest, which will have them flipping pages until the end and eagerly anticipating the next installment."
—*Library Journal* (starred review)

"Uplifting . . . a cliffhanger ending for Jo Marie begs for a swift resolution in the next book." —*Kirkus Reviews*

Rose Harbor in Bloom

"[Debbie Macomber] draws in threads of her earlier book in this series, *The Inn at Rose Harbor,* in what is likely to be just as comfortable a place for Macomber fans as for Jo Marie's guests at the inn." —*The Seattle Times*

"Macomber's legions of fans will embrace this cozy, heartwarming read." —*Booklist*

"Readers will find the emotionally impactful storylines and sweet, redemptive character arcs for which the author is famous. Classic Macomber, which will please fans and keep them coming back for more." —*Kirkus Reviews*

"The storybook scenery of lighthouses, cozy bed and breakfast inns dotting the coastline, and seagulls flying above takes readers on personal journeys of first love, lost love and recaptured love, [presenting] love in its purest and most personal forms."
—*Bookreporter*

The Inn at Rose Harbor

"Debbie Macomber's Cedar Cove romance novels have a warm, comfy feel to them. Perhaps that's why they've sold millions."
—*USA Today*

"Debbie Macomber has written a charming, cathartic romance full of tasteful passion and good sense. Reading it is a lot like enjoying comfort food, as you know the book will end well and leave you feeling pleasant and content. The tone is warm and serene, and the characters are likeable yet realistic. . . . *The Inn at Rose Harbor* is a wonderful novel that will keep the reader's undivided attention." —*Bookreporter*

"The prolific Macomber introduces a spin-off of sorts from her popular Cedar Cove series, still set in that fictional small town but centered on Jo Marie Rose, a youngish widow who buys and operates the bed and breakfast of the title. This clever premise allows Macomber to craft stories around the B&B's guests, Abby and Josh in this inaugural effort, while using Jo Marie and her ongoing recovery from the death of her husband Paul in Afghanistan as the series' anchor. . . . With her characteristic optimism, Macomber provides fresh starts for both."
—*Booklist*

"Emotionally charged romance." —*Kirkus Reviews*

BLOSSOM STREET

Blossom Street Brides

"A wonderful, love-affirming novel . . . an engaging, emotionally fulfilling story that clearly shows why [Macomber] is a peerless storyteller." —*Examiner.com*

"Rewarding . . . Macomber amply delivers her signature engrossing relationship tales, wrapping her readers in warmth as fuzzy and soft as a hand-knitted creation from everyone's favorite yarn shop." —*Bookreporter*

"Fans will happily return to the warm, welcoming sanctuary of Macomber's Blossom Street, catching up with old friends from past Blossom Street books and meeting new ones being welcomed into the fold." —*Kirkus Reviews*

"Macomber's nondenominational-inspirational women's novel, with its large cast of characters, will resonate with fans of the popular series." —*Booklist*

Starting Now

"Macomber understands the often complex nature of a woman's friendships, as well as the emotional language women use with their friends." —*NY Journal of Books*

"There is a reason that legions of Macomber fans ask for more Blossom Street books. They fully engage her readers as her characters discover happiness, purpose, and meaning in life. . . . Macomber's feel-good novel, emphasizing interpersonal relationships and putting people above status and objects, is truly satisfying." —*Booklist* (starred review)

"Macomber's writing and storytelling deliver what she's famous for—a smooth, satisfying tale with characters her fans will cheer for and an arc that is cozy, heartwarming and ends with the expected happily-ever-after." —*Kirkus Reviews*

CHRISTMAS NOVELS

Jingle All the Way

"[*Jingle All the Way*] will leave readers feeling merry and bright."
—*Publishers Weekly*

"This delightful Christmas story can be enjoyed any time of the year." —*New York Journal of Books*

A Mrs. Miracle Christmas

"This sweet, inspirational story . . . had enough dramatic surprises to keep pages turning."
—*Library Journal* (starred review)

"Anyone who enjoys Christmas will appreciate this sparkling snow globe of a story." —*Publishers Weekly*

Alaskan Holiday

"Picture-perfect . . . this charmer will please Macomber fans and newcomers alike." —*Publishers Weekly*

"[A] tender romance lightly brushed with holiday magic."
—*Library Journal*

"[A] thoroughly charming holiday romance." —*Booklist*

Mr. Miracle

"[Macomber] writes about romance, family and friendship with a gentle, humorous touch." —*Tampa Bay Times*

"Macomber spins another sweet, warmhearted holiday tale that will be as comforting to her fans as hot chocolate on Christmas morning." —*Kirkus Reviews*

"This gentle, inspiring romance will be a sought-after read."
—*Library Journal*

Starry Night

"Contemporary romance queen Macomber hits the sweet spot with this tender tale of impractical love. . . . A delicious Christmas miracle well worth waiting for."
—*Publishers Weekly* (starred review)

"[A] holiday confection . . . as much a part of the season for some readers as cookies and candy canes." —*Kirkus Reviews*

Angels at the Table

"Rings in Christmas in tried-and-true Macomber style, with romance and a touch of heavenly magic." —*Kirkus Reviews*

"[A] sweetly charming holiday romance." —*Library Journal*

Christmas 2022

Dear Friends,

Merry Christmas! One of many aspects I enjoy as an author is plotting sessions with my writing friends. The idea for this book came about when Linda Nichols and I were discussing the plot for her next story. Her storyline revolved around two people who were complete opposites. As so often happens when we're together, we were joking and laughing while we bounced ideas around. I don't recall who suggested the pastor and the bartender, but the story potential instantly grabbed hold of my imagination. What would happen if they traded places? Linda had a different situation in mind, and we continued discussing her plotline. But the more I thought about the pastor and the bartender, the stronger the idea blossomed in my mind.

Rarely have I enjoyed writing a book more. There are times when a story is so compelling, so strong in my mind, that I can barely sleep. All I can think about is getting back to my computer so I can continue writing. Just as often, there are books where I feel the weight of each word and scene. *The Christmas Spirit* was different in that it was a complete joy to write from beginning to end. I don't think I've laughed more in any other book I've ever written.

My hope is that you will enjoy reading this fun book. I hope you feel the cheer of the holiday season as Nana tells the story, the very real story of the pastor and the bartender who traded jobs the week before Christmas.

Debbie Macomber

P.S. For those keen *Monday Night Football* fans, the game described in the story actually took place on December 12, 1977, and not the week of Christmas.

The Christmas Spirit

DEBBIE MACOMBER

The Christmas Spirit

A Novel

BALLANTINE BOOKS

NEW YORK

The Christmas Spirit is a work of fiction. Names, characters,
places, and incidents are the products of the author's imagination
or are used fictitiously. Any resemblance to actual events, locales,
or persons, living or dead, is entirely coincidental.

2023 Ballantine Books Mass Market Edition

Copyright © 2022 by Debbie Macomber
Excerpt from *The Perfect Holiday* by Debbie Macomber
copyright © 2023 by Debbie Macomber

Published in the United States by Ballantine Books, an imprint of
Random House, a division of Penguin Random House LLC, New York.

BALLANTINE is a registered trademark and the colophon is a trademark of
Penguin Random House LLC.

Originally published in hardcover in the United States by
Ballantine Books, an imprint of Random House, a division of
Penguin Random House LLC, in 2022.

This book contains an excerpt from the forthcoming book
The Perfect Holiday by Debbie Macomber. This excerpt has been set
for this edition only and may not reflect the final content of
the forthcoming edition.

ISBN 978-0-593-50012-5
Ebook ISBN 978-0-593-50011-8

Cover design: Belina Huey
Cover illustration: Tom Hallman, based on images by Alamy (street),
Shutterstock (gazebo), and Depositphotos (puppies)

Printed in the United States of America

randomhousebooks.com

2 4 6 8 9 7 5 3 1

Title-page and chapter-opener art: LenLis © Adobe Stock Photos

Ballantine Books mass market edition: October 2023

To
Linda Nichols
Author, knitter, and, best of all,
a precious friend

The Christmas Spirit

Prologue

"Nana, Nana, we're here," eight-year-old Lance shouted, as he raced into the house ahead of his six-year-old sister. He launched himself into her open arms, as if it had been weeks since they'd last spent time together. Lance and Lily visited often, and their Nana treasured each and every minute with her precious grandchildren.

"Are we baking cookies again?" Lance asked, the instant she released him. He eyed the kitchen for signs of his favorite activity.

"I don't want to bake cookies," Lily said with a pout, following her warm hug. "I want Nana to tell us another story. Nana's stories are the best. Besides, Mom says Lance eats too many cookies."

"That he does," Nana agreed, ruffling her grandson's

hair. "It's late and Nana is tired, so let's settle down with hot chocolate and a story." She'd had a long, hard day, distributing food baskets to families in need, in addition to a lengthy practice with the church choir as they prepared for the Christmas Eve service. A smile came over her as she recalled another Christmas program many years ago, one that would likely never be forgotten.

Lance cocked his head as if giving the idea consideration. "A story's okay, as long as there's no kissing."

"I like kissing," Lily argued, looking up at her nana as if to assure her that any story she told, kissing or not, was fine by her.

After making cocoa, including marshmallows, they moved into the living room and sat on the big sofa in front of the fireplace, mugs in hand. A gentle fire flickered, warming the room. Several red stockings with white fluffy cuffs were strung across the mantel, where a crèche was placed. The bright paint on the figures had faded to pastel colors over the years. Still, it remained a family treasure, handed down from one generation to the next.

After taking sips of their drinks, both children snuggled up against her side. Nana placed her arm around her granddaughter's shoulders as Lily leaned against her grandmother. Lance pressed his head against her arm as they settled in for an engaging tale.

"Nana, can I start?" Lily asked. "The beginning is my favorite part. Once upon a time . . ."

"Once upon a time," Lance echoed, clearly not enthused. "Not again, please, Nana, make this a real story."

"All right, I will," Nana said.

"It won't be a once-upon-a-time story?" Lily asked, with a sad face.

"No, this story is even better."

"How can it be better?" Lily asked. "Fairy tales always start that way."

"Remember, Sweet Pea, this isn't a fairy tale. This is a real story." Nana kissed the top of Lily's head. "But it's a good one. I promise. Probably one of the best stories I've ever shared."

"But if it doesn't start with *once upon a time*, then how does it start?"

Before she could answer, Lance asked, "Is there kissing?"

Nana hesitated, not wanting to mislead her grandson. "Some."

"Goodie." Lily clapped her hands.

Bending her head close to Lance, Nana whispered, "You can cover your ears when I get to that part if you want."

Lance released a deep sigh. "Okay, but let me know ahead of time."

"I will," she promised.

Because he was still unsure, Lance asked again, "You're sure this isn't one of those silly fairy tales?"

"I'm sure," Nana said. "This story starts out *in the beginning.*"

"Oh, I like it already," Lily said, snuggling all the closer.

Nana paused to regard her grandson. "Is that better?" she asked him.

Lance's wary look suggested he remained skeptical.

"Go on, Nana," Lily urged, "tell us more."

Nana relaxed her back against the cushioned sofa and closed her eyes as the memories rolled through her mind. A slow smile came over her as she started the story.

"In the beginning there were two rough-and-tough friends named—"

"Can I name them?" Lily interrupted to ask. "You let me name the people in once-upon-a-time stories."

"All right, Lily you can name one, and Lance can name the other."

Lily didn't pause. "Since this is an in-the-beginning story, I want to name him after Uncle Peter."

Nana smiled. "That's thoughtful of you, Sweet Pea, and that is the perfect name. What about you, Lance? Do you have a name in mind?"

"Hank," Lance said automatically. "After Grandpa Hank."

Nana approved. "You couldn't have chosen better."

"Is this story about the two of them because they're good friends?"

"You'll have to wait and see."

Lily and Lance smiled at each other. Naming the characters was one of the fun aspects of Nana's stories, which was why she let them do it.

"Okay, back to the story," she said. "The two men named Peter and Hank had been friends nearly their entire lives. They grew up together, attended the same schools, both played football, and both ran track. Peter was the star quarterback, and Hank was the fastest runner on the cross-country team."

"That's what I'm talking about." Lance's face brightened as he pumped his fist in the air.

"Did they fall in love and marry their sweethearts?" Lily asked.

"Nana, please, don't ruin the story." Lance closed his eyes and bounced against the back of the sofa, dismayed already.

Nana ignored them both. "After graduating from high school, Peter went away to college, and Hank took over the tavern from his father after he retired." She paused and saw that Lance was already involved in the tale, and Lily was patiently waiting for the romance. "But like in the fairy tales, this all took place long ago, before there were cell phones and social media."

"That long ago?" Lance cried. "Did they live in caves?"

Nana smiled. "No, not caves. They lived in houses. They had phones, but the phones stayed inside, and most were attached to the wall. The ones that weren't on the wall were much too big to carry."

Both children regarded her with wide eyes.

"Now back to the story," Nana said. "Peter and Hank were the very best of friends, even after they left school."

"My best friend is Everett," Lance said. "We're gonna be friends like that even when we're old and out of school."

"I bet you will," Nana said. "Even after Peter graduated from college, he routinely spent time with Hank, and that's where the story really begins."

CHAPTER ONE

1977

"Hey, man, sorry I'm late," Hank said, as he slid into the red upholstered booth at Mom's Place across from his best friend. He was running on less than five hours' sleep, and his day was only getting started. "Did I keep you waiting long?"

"No, I was late myself." Pete had always been the responsible, prompt one. It surprised Hank to learn his pastor friend could be late for anything.

The waitress came with a coffeepot, and both men turned over the beige mugs to be filled. Pete smiled at her as she handed them menus and then swiftly left. Hank noticed how Pete's gaze lingered over the waitress as she returned to the counter and refilled another customer's cup.

"I'm telling you, these long hours are killing me," Hank said, as he wiped a hand down his face. His eyes burned, and he couldn't remember the last time he'd had a decent meal. As different as they were, they had continued a friendship after Pete had graduated from seminary and returned to Bridgeport. Pete looked every bit the pastor with his clean-cut looks, while Hank was often mistaken for a hippie, with his long hair and the casual way he dressed. Scruffy jeans and a T-shirt were his standard uniform, whereas he suspected his friend hadn't worn blue jeans since his college days.

Hank was the owner, manager, bartender, and chief bottle washer for the tavern The Last Call. Mom's Place, where they routinely met for lunch every month or so, was halfway between their two towns, Pete in Bridgeport and Hank in Kettle Springs. "I didn't get away from the tavern until after two this morning. Some days I swear I get less than three or four hours' sleep a night. This job's a killer."

Pete glanced up from the menu. "I thought you loved the tavern."

"I do. I always knew I'd be taking Dad's place one day. I looked forward to it. The regulars are great and keep me in the black, but I have no life. I haven't been on a date in six months."

"I'd think you'd meet women left and right," Pete said, before taking a sip of his coffee.

"I do. Lots of great women. I thought I'd be married and have a couple kids by the time I hit thirty."

"Why aren't you?" Pete asked.

Clearly, Hank's lifelong friend had no understanding of what managing a tavern entailed. "There's a big difference between meeting lots of women and having time to actually date. I work fourteen hours a day and sometimes longer."

Pete frowned. "Hire someone."

Hank snorted. Pete made it sound easy. "Do you have any idea how hard it is to find good help these days? I tried taking on a part-time bartender, and he drank all my profits. It's a slim enough profit margin as it is. At the rate he was drinking, I was about to go out of business. The thing is, if I need to be there to keep an eye on the staff, I might as well do without."

After a brief hesitation, Pete acknowledged Hank's dilemma: "Gotcha."

"Having my own business takes every spare minute I have. If I'm not at the bar serving drinks, then I'm in the office doing paperwork. Keeping up on the orders or dealing with the taxes. I swear it's one headache after another. Do you have any idea how much effort goes into the accounting aspect of being a business owner?"

"Well, yes . . ."

"Oh, come on." Hank gave a short laugh. "You're a pastor. The church doesn't pay taxes or struggle with money hassles."

Pete nearly spewed the coffee out of his mouth. "You have no idea! Pastoring a church is no walk in the park."

"Are you joking?" Hank was about to say more when they were interrupted by the waitress. He swallowed his argument and turned his attention back to deciding what he wanted for lunch.

Pad in hand, the young woman asked, "What can I get you gentlemen?"

Without looking up from the plastic-coated menu, Hank said, "I'll take the soup-and-sandwich special. On wheat, hold the tomato."

The waitress wrote it down, and he handed her the menu. Next, she looked to Pete.

"I'd like the chef salad," he said, "with Thousand Island dressing."

"I'll get that order in right away," she said, as she turned toward the kitchen.

"She's cute," Pete said, watching the young woman in the pink uniform with the white apron.

Hank frowned, his thoughts still on all he was missing in life. He caught his friend's interest in the young waitress, though, and played along. "Who's cute?"

"The waitress. It isn't any wonder you don't date. You

aren't paying attention. That woman is beautiful, and I noticed there wasn't a ring on her finger, either."

Pete was paying attention. Still, Hank let the comment pass. Pete should be the one married by now. He lived the good life and had none of the worries that hounded Hank from day to day. Hank envied him in that way.

Before Hank could encourage him to ask the waitress for a date, Pete said, "You should know my life isn't anything like you assume."

"Are you kidding me? Come on, Pete. You work your own hours . . ."

"That's not exactly true."

Hank dismissed his objection with a wave of his hand. "You get a steady paycheck every month."

"Yes, but . . ."

Hank wasn't listening. "Plus, the church provides you with your own house. No mortgage payments, no worries about making ends meet. And to top it off, you only need to make an appearance once a week. You're living the life, man."

Pete simply shook his head. It looked as if he was about to argue when the waitress returned with their lunch.

Again, Hank noticed the way his friend watched the young woman. It left him to wonder aloud, "Why is it you've never married?"

"Me?" Pete asked, as he mixed the salad and the dressing together.

"Yeah, you. Seeing how you made such a big deal about how easy it is for me to meet women, what about you?"

Pete looked like a deer in the headlights and then like a fish out of water, his mouth opening and closing several times.

"Not so easy to find the right one, is it?" Hank said, understanding all too well. "Church has gotta be full of upright, single, Christian women. You could have your pick of any one of them."

"I suppose," Pete reluctantly agreed. "The truth is, I don't know why I'm still single. I've had plenty of opportunity to date, but I've yet to find that special someone."

"I bet Gracie has something to say about that," Hank commented. Hank and Pete's sister had been at odds for years, always rubbing each other the wrong way. God save him from opinionated women. She was a spitfire, that's for sure. Frankly, Hank couldn't imagine how Pete worked with Gracie as his church secretary. She didn't have the personality for it, as far as he could figure.

"Gracie is Gracie," Pete said. "She's as righteous as ever. Stubborn as a mule and loyal as a dog."

"That sounds about right," Hank said with a snort. He smiled just thinking about her. She had her nose in the air and a holier-than-thou attitude. It was no surprise she hadn't married, either. Pete was nothing like his sister. His personality was perfect for his life's work. He was a caring, thoughtful man. Wise. Full of faith. Not that Hank lacked faith. He was square with God. But being a Christian didn't require him to show up for church every Sunday.

"You should know my job isn't all that wonderful, Hank. I have my own set of problems," Pete said.

"Sure you do," he said offhandedly. He didn't mean to sound condescending, but Pete had no concept of the demands on Hank's time and finances.

"It's Christmas in less than a week," Pete continued. "I'm running ragged getting everything organized. You, on the other hand . . ."

"What about me?"

"You party every night—"

"It's not a party," Hank interrupted. "I work hard to create a fun atmosphere but trust me it isn't always a party."

"So you say. You may work a lot of hours, which I don't discount, but you can sleep in each morning."

"Dream on," Hank said and rolled his eyes.

"And while you claim you don't have any time to date, which I have trouble believing, you have a chance every night to meet women."

"You have no idea what being a tavern owner means!"

"And you have no idea what the life of a pastor is like."

Hank laughed. "You couldn't do my job for a week."

Pete snickered. "You couldn't do *my* job for a week."

"Give me a break. You're living the easy life."

Pete set his fork down and leaned forward, his eyes intense. "You ready to find out?"

"What do you mean?"

"Fine, since you think I've got it so easy, let's trade places. I'll work at the bar and you fill in for me at the church."

Hank didn't hesitate. This was like taking candy from a baby. "You're on." He thrust his hand across the table. Pete extended his own hand and the two shook.

"Starting when?" Hank asked.

Pete's smile was wide. "No time like the present."

Oh, this was going to be good, Hank mused. Monday night. He was going to put his feet up and watch *Monday Night Football,* and for the first time in longer than he could remember. Better yet, he'd be able to pay attention to what was happening on the field.

Life didn't get any sweeter than this, and his friend was about to learn the biggest lesson of his life.

CHAPTER TWO

Grace Ann Armstrong glanced up from the typewriter when her brother returned from his lunch with Hank Colfax. Personally, she didn't know what it was about the tavern owner that appealed to Peter. Hank was the one who first shortened her brother's name to Pete, and soon all his friends followed, much to her consternation. As far as she could see, the two men had nothing in common, nothing that should bond their friendship, other than the fact that years ago they'd once played on the same football team and ran cross-country together.

Bottom line—Grace Ann didn't trust Hank. He was a tease and a flirt, and she wanted nothing to do with him when she was in high school, and even less so now. She did her best to hide her prejudice, although it was difficult not to share her opinion of her brother's best friend. The one time she couldn't help herself hadn't gone well. Grace Ann hadn't brought up Hank's name again.

"How was your lunch?" she asked, as Peter headed for his desk in the church office.

"Fabulous," he mumbled, sounding distracted. "What's my schedule like for the rest of the week?"

Grace Ann reached for the appointment book and reviewed Peter's commitments. "You're scheduled to pick up the mule from the Martin residence for the live Nativity scene. The Carney family is lending you their horse trailer."

"Why so early?"

"The Martins are leaving to visit their children. You promised to take Hortense for the week in exchange for her being part of the live Nativity on Christmas Eve."

Peter smiled, his eyes sparkling like he couldn't wait to pick up Hortense. "Wonderful."

That was an odd response. All those extra hours were sure to drain Peter's energy. "And of course, this is the week to deliver the charity food baskets, and then there's your regular visitation. Mrs. Millstone especially asked to see you this week. I set that up for tomorrow." That old battle-ax was a piece of work. How Peter maintained his patience with the woman was beyond Grace Ann. It was important that they pander to the former schoolteacher, as she had promised a hefty donation toward replacing the church roof, which was badly in need of it.

He arched his brows. "Right on." His smile grew even bigger before he slapped his knee and chuckled. "This should be good."

Grace Ann frowned and asked, "What's going on?"

"Nothing"—he hesitated—"of importance. I'll explain in a moment. Continue." He waved his hand, encouraging her to finish reviewing his calendar.

With each appointment she mentioned, her brother seemed to find nothing but delight. He couldn't seem to stop smiling and chuckling to himself.

"Anything else?"

"Well, yes, there's the possibility of a finance committee meeting. It was delayed last week because of the snowstorm. The last time I talked to Leonard, he insinuated it could wait until after Christmas."

For the first time since his return from lunch, Peter frowned. "Yes, make sure to delay that meeting until after Christmas."

"Okay, if Leonard phones, I'll let him know you want to put it off." Church finances were always a worry for her brother. She personally knew of twice in the last year when he'd taken less of a salary in order to meet the church budget. Grace Ann had offered to do without herself, but Peter wouldn't hear of it.

"That's it, then?"

"Yes." She glanced down at the appointment book to make sure she hadn't forgotten anything. "For now, anyway." As the week progresses, and seeing that Christmas fell on a Sunday, it would be double duty. Christmas Eve on Saturday night and then another church service on Sunday morning.

"Great," he said, when she'd finished. "It's going to be a busy week."

"Every week is busy." Peter was often exhausted by the end of the day. More than once, Grace Ann had encouraged him to find a helpmate. She did what she could to make his life easier. She was his sister, though, and what Peter really needed was a wife.

Grace Ann had lost count of the number of single women from the church she felt would be perfect for her brother. Godly women. He'd thoughtfully listened to her suggestions and had dated a couple of those she considered worthy candidates. Nothing clicked. She was discouraged, and it'd been a month since she'd last offered up another name. After all this time, she had no idea what Peter sought in a wife, because clearly they didn't share the same criteria.

One reason for her hesitation was Peter's interest in why she herself hadn't married. The majority of women at the age of twenty-eight in their community were married with children. A handful of the girls in her high school class had married the summer following gradua-tion. After what had happened with Ken, she rarely dated. It was harder to meet single men in a small town. That, however, was only a small part of why she remained single. She wasn't about to marry just because that was what women her age were expected to do.

At the first of the year, she'd made a list of everything she wanted in a husband. She'd made the mistake of showing it to Peter, thinking it would help him in his own quest to find a wife. Her brother had read over her crite-ria, laughed softly, and then smiled before commenting, "It looks to me like you want to marry Jesus."

Grace Ann hadn't been amused.

"What are you up to this week?" he asked, cutting into her thoughts.

"Me?" she asked, surprised by the question. "This isn't an employee review, is it?" Peter would need to search far and wide to find anyone more dedicated to serving the church than she was.

"Not at all," he assured her, leaning against the side of her desk, as he looked over her side of the appointment book.

"Well, other than overseeing the office and answering phones, there's choir practice Wednesday evening." Hold-ing her finger on the page, she glanced up. "It would be good for you to make a showing. The choir has given a lot of extra hours to ensure that the Christmas Eve service is everything it should be."

"I'll be more than happy to see to that." He nodded approvingly, as if adding an extra assignment to his schedule was exactly what he longed to hear. This was all so strange. Something was definitely up, but Peter was being tight-lipped.

"There's a Ladies Missionary Society meeting on Thursday." As president of the guild, Grace Ann had worked tirelessly to support those in the mission field. Both their parents were currently church planting in Costa Rica, dedicating themselves to the work of the Lord following retirement. Grace Ann was proud of her efforts, and the efforts of the other women of the church who'd given so much of themselves.

"I'll be cleaning the church before the service, of course." That was part of her regular duties. Peter often stepped in to lend a hand, which she appreciated.

"Put me down for that, will you?"

"Thank you, Peter." She found cleaning the toilets in the men's bathroom a challenge. The male youths were often off target when it came to their aim. Her brother had taken pity on her and had volunteered for the task, for which Grace Ann was most grateful.

"Make sure there's easy access to all the songbooks," he added.

"Of course." Naturally, Peter wanted everything perfect for the Christmas Eve service. Several in the community showed up at church only for Christmas and then Easter, as if that was enough religion to save their souls. Sort of like getting fire insurance before they met the Grim Reaper.

"I'll wipe down all the pews, too." Everything would be as spotless as she could make it. Grace Ann took her job seriously.

Peter showed his appreciation with an encouraging smile. Her brother was a gentle soul, caring and kind, unlike some friends of his she could mention. One in particular. She deeply admired her brother's Christian spirit, his willingness to dig in and give liberally of his time and himself. It wasn't beyond him to help those in need. He never complained or questioned when others called on him. He had a generosity of spirit she admired and often wished she could be more like him.

"I'll need you to type up a list of what's required of me for each day," Peter said, with what resembled a smug look.

This was the first time he'd ever asked her to do such a thing. They spoke each morning and reviewed the day's commitments as soon as they arrived at the church office, precisely at eight.

"Do you plan on being gone from the office?" she asked, thinking that had to be the reason for his request.

"As a matter of fact, I will be."

This was an unusual development, and one that came as a shock. "Where will you be?"

"Kettle Springs." His eyes sparkled with delight.

"Kettle Springs," Grace Ann repeated. "Why would you want to go to Kettle Springs?" Then it came to her. She should have guessed her brother's less-than-desirable friend had cooked up some dodgy scheme that would involve Peter.

"This has to do with Hank, doesn't it?"

"You could say that."

Exactly as she thought.

Whatever it was appeared to please Peter. Her brother was all smiles. Knowing him as well as she did, she noticed he seemed to be holding back the need to laugh, as if this was some sort of comedy in the making.

"Peter. Tell me. What's going on?" Whatever it was, Grace Ann was convinced she wasn't going to like it.

"I'll be tending Hank's bar."

"You're doing what?" She already knew this was going to be trouble.

"I'm going to work as a bartender for the rest of the week. Of course, I'll return in time for the service Christmas Eve and Christmas morning. Don't look so worried. This is going to work out beautifully."

"You can't do this, Peter. It's impossible." God help

them if anyone from the church learned about this. "Hank put you up to this, didn't he? Don't bother to deny it. This is exactly the kind of thing that . . . that Neanderthal would do."

"You worry too much," he said again, as if this was of little significance.

"Peter, you should seriously consider what you're doing." She needed a moment to clear the shock of this from her mind to help her brother understand the ramifications of this decision. "What if one of the church members hears of this?" She blurted out the first thing that crowded to the forefront of her objections. Peter simply had to listen to reason.

"What if they do?" he asked, completely unconcerned.

Her brother had lost his mind. She was astonished that he would be so blind to the risk he seemed all too willing to take. "You could lose your position."

"That's doubtful. Come on, Grace Ann, you're over-reacting. It's only for a few days in another town twenty miles away. It's unlikely I'll run into someone from Bridgeport, and even if I do, so what?"

With her mind spinning, Grace Ann pressed her hand against her brow as if to help her sort through all the thoughts bouncing around inside her head. Her brother was delusional and required help. This was crazy, and from the look of him, she'd rarely seen him more excited.

"Do you think people who come into a tavern don't need God in their lives?"

"But . . ."

"It's the perfect opportunity for me to meet people who wouldn't ordinarily attend church."

"Ah . . ."

"Grace Ann, you're looking pale all of a sudden. Do you need some air?"

What she needed was for her brother to tell her this was all part of some silly joke. From the way he studied her, she could see that wasn't about to happen.

"I don't know what Hank said to convince you to commit professional suicide." Peter's friend was a constant source of irritation, and always had been from the time they were in grade school. He'd insisted on calling her Gracie, even though he knew she detested the name. This, though . . . this was above and beyond, she couldn't let Peter do it, for his own sake and the sake of his ministry.

"What about your duties here at the church?" Peter couldn't meet the needs of the church and at the same time work at The Last Call. It wasn't humanly possible.

"I've got that covered."

He'd found a substitute pastor? That seemed highly unlikely, especially at this late date. "Who's going to fill in for you?" she asked.

"Hank."

The breath left her lungs. Even before she could find the oxygen to breathe again, Grace Ann started shaking her head. This couldn't be happening. Hank serving as a pastor . . . She couldn't think of anyone less qualified.

"You're joking, right?" She sincerely prayed she'd misunderstood him and this was all part of a bad dream. If so, she wanted to wake up soon.

"No joke. I know Hank isn't your favorite person."

Her brother had no idea.

"How? Why?" At first, she'd assumed Hank had asked Peter to fill in as a favor. As an emergency.

"It'll be fine," her brother said soothingly. "We're trading places for a few days, that's all."

"That's all?" she repeated, too stunned to say anything more.

This was a disaster in the making and she wanted no part of it.

CHAPTER THREE

Hank relaxed against the sofa and rested his feet on the ottoman, crossing his ankles. What a treat to have *Monday Night Football* all to himself. Mondays were as busy as weekend nights at The Last Call during the football season. He was often run ragged, filling orders, delivering pitchers of beer, and doing his best to keep everyone happy. Rarely did he get a chance to actually enjoy watching the game. This was about as close to heaven as he was likely to get. Football, uninterrupted. Yup, life didn't get much better.

His afternoon had been busy. Pete showed up at the tavern a couple hours after they'd left Mom's Place. He'd stopped off at the church to collect his things before reconvening with Hank. The better part of what was left of the afternoon was spent with Hank showing Pete the ropes. He almost felt guilty leaving Pete alone. But a deal was a deal.

Howard Cosell's familiar face showed on the television screen, along with Don Meredith, as the commentators for the game between the Dallas Cowboys and the San Francisco 49ers. There'd been a lot of talk about the Cowboys player Tony Dorsett, and Hank was eager to see the running back in action.

Seattle had gotten a football franchise the year before, and their games were the highlight of the week. It'd changed Sundays at The Last Call. Jim Zorn, the Seahawks' quarterback, and his favorite receiver, Steve Largent, were Seattle royalty. Hank knew a few guys from Bridgeport who were lucky enough to get tickets to a game at the Kingdome. There'd been talk of little else after their return. Seattle was definitely in the big time and had been ever since the World's Fair was held there in 1962.

Hank wasn't surprised by how neat and orderly Pete's house was. He felt a bit guilty because his own place, above the tavern, was a mess, with dirty clothes littering the floor, though he did his best to put it in order before Pete arrived. With so much else to do to prepare for the switch, he'd barely made a dent. Dirty dishes filled the sink. He couldn't remember the last time he'd done any real housecleaning. Pete hadn't complained, although he had every right to expect clean sheets and a made bed.

By contrast, the parsonage was spic and span: almost as if the only time Pete spent there was to sleep.

Other than the list of duties Pete had handed him, the one bit of advice his friend had given was about Gracie.

"You should know Grace isn't keen on this idea."

"I didn't think she would be." Hank could easily picture Gracie's pursed lips when Pete told her about their agreement.

"Go gentle with her," Pete had advised.

"Of course." Hank planned to stay as far removed from Gracie as he could manage.

"She means well," Pete added.

"Sure, she does," Hank had said, and struggled to disguise his sarcasm. Never in all his days had he met anyone more self-righteous than Grace Ann Armstrong. The woman had her nose so far up in the air that she was in danger of drowning in a rainstorm.

The phone in the kitchen rang. Hank's gaze momentarily left the television screen. The Cowboys had just gotten their first touchdown, and nothing was going to tear him away from the game. Besides, it was after five and he was off-duty. Whoever was calling would need to get in touch with the church office in the morning.

After nine persistent rings—he counted them—whoever

was calling thankfully gave up. *Good.* The noise was an irritant and made it difficult for Hank to follow Howard Cosell as he reviewed the plays on the field.

Ten minutes later, someone came knocking on the door. Whomever it was needed to calm down. The pounding was hard enough to break down the front door.

"All right, all right," he muttered, as he uncrossed his ankles and left the cozy sofa to answer.

Gracie stood on the front porch, her dark brown hair wet and dripping from the sleet and rain. She glared at him with such a fierce look it was a wonder she didn't drill holes straight into his torso.

"Gracie," he greeted cheerfully, as if he'd waited all night for the opportunity to see her. His smile was wide, despite her obvious displeasure.

"My name is Grace Ann," she reminded him, irritation emanating from her in waves.

While it was tempting to rile her and ignore the comment, he could see she was already angry. Remembering Pete's advice, he resisted the urge to aggravate her further. "Come in. You must be freezing standing out there."

"No, thank you."

It was apparent she hadn't come to bring him a casserole or welcome him. "What can I do for you?" he asked, remaining pleasant. The truth was, he found her attitude amusing. She took life far too seriously. He wondered if she ever allowed herself to kick back and have a bit of fun. He remembered how in high school she wore her hair in one long braid down the middle of her back. That braid was more temptation than he could resist. He'd tugged it at every opportunity. Her outrage had amused him. That braid was long gone now, but those piercing blue eyes of hers hadn't changed. One look could turn a man to stone.

He'd always thought she was pretty, or she could be if he was able to look past her holier-than-thou attitude. Unlike her brother, she was petite. Barely an inch or two above five feet. Pete was six feet if he was an inch. Same hair and eyes.

At one point in his senior year, despite her apparent dislike of him, Hank had been tempted to ask Gracie out on a date. He hadn't because he knew she'd likely refuse. As Pete said, Gracie was as stubborn as a mule and as loyal as a dog. In Hank's way of thinking, Gracie was so heavenly minded, she was no earthly good. Life was black and white for her, unlike Pete, whose real gift was understanding human nature and accepting others for exactly who they were. Pete was never one to cram faith down anyone's throat. He loved people, and anyone who spent time with him, even a short while, recognized as much.

"You didn't answer the phone," Gracie accused him, as if he were on trial and standing before a judge.

"Well, no, I figured if it was an emergency, whomever it was would call back." That was fudging the truth a bit. Honesty, however, wasn't likely to gain Gracie's approval. He hadn't wanted to answer for fear he'd miss an important play. San Francisco had scored and this was proving to be a well-matched, highly anticipated game. Hank didn't intend to miss a single minute.

"Did my brother give you the list?" she demanded, with a tone that would have made a drill sergeant proud.

"He did. Come inside, Gracie, before you catch a cold. I don't bite."

"I'd rather not. Getting back to this list."

"Yes, I have it. Pete dutifully handed it to me." He glanced over his shoulder at the television, longing to return.

"Did you read it?"

Gracie had missed her calling. She'd make a great prosecutor. "Well, if you must know—"

"Obviously you didn't," she said, cutting him off.

"To be fair, there was a lot of instruction I had to give Pete before he took over as bartender. He didn't have a chance to review his list with me."

"And you didn't take the time to read it yourself."

The crowd in Candlestick Park in San Francisco went wild. Hank looked longingly over his shoulder and saw the score. The 49ers had made the field goal, and he'd missed the play. It was hard to hold back a groan.

"Whatever it is, can it wait until tomorrow?" he asked.

"No." For emphasis she stomped her foot. "You were due to collect Hortense more than an hour ago."

What in the name of all that was holy was she talking about? "Who's Hortense?"

"Farmer Martin's mule."

Hank scratched the side of his head. "Can you tell me why I would venture out in the sleet and rain to collect a mule?"

"If you read the list . . ."

"Which I didn't, so you'll need to fill me in."

Gracie sighed and lowered her head to stare at her feet as though she was at the end of her patience. "I knew this wasn't going to work. You're not to be trusted. I told Peter this was a huge mistake, but would he listen to me? Oh no. He seems to think—"

"Just tell me what I need to do, and I'll do it." Hank cut her off before she could continue with this tirade, which she seemed keen on doing.

"We need Hortense for the live Nativity on Christmas Eve."

"This is Monday and Christmas Eve is Saturday," he felt obliged to remind her.

"There are extenuating circumstances; you need to collect Hortense tonight. It's all explained on the list."

"Okay. Tell me where I need to go to claim this mule and I'll take care of it first thing in the morning." He started to close the door, when Gracie stuck her foot in the way, preventing him from escaping.

Gracie stood glaring at him with her hands akimbo. "It has to be done tonight."

"Tonight?" He inwardly groaned. "Why?"

"Because," she said, as if making these explanations was trying her patience, "the Carney family leaves tomorrow morning."

"Wait," he said, and held up his hand. "I thought you said Farmer Martin has Hortense?"

"He does. But Mr. Martin doesn't have a horse trailer, so you'll need to collect that from the Carney family, get Hortense and bring her to town, and then return the horse trailer to the Carneys."

Hank's head went spinning. "I have no idea where these people live, Gracie."

"Don't call me Gracie."

"Sorry." He wasn't, but admitting as much would do him no favors. So much for enjoying *Monday Night Football*. He should have known this was too good to be true. The fates were against him.

"You'll do it?" She sounded shocked, as if she'd expected an argument.

"Is there anyone else who can?"

"Not this late."

As hard as it was to admit, Gracie was right. "I should have paid more attention to this list."

"Yes, you should have."

"My apologies, Gracie . . . I mean Grace Ann."

"You apologize?" Surprise lit up her face, and once again, he was reminded what an attractive woman she was, or could be if she'd loosen up a bit.

"Yes, I didn't take Pete's duties seriously. The thing is, I don't know where to find the farm where Hortense is, let alone where the Carneys live. Would you be willing to come with me?"

Gracie's mouth opened and closed twice, as if that was the last thing she'd expected him to suggest.

"I . . ."

"Otherwise, Hortense will have to wait until the morning, and as you reminded me, the Carneys need their horse trailer come morning."

"Yes, I understand, but—"

"It's pitch-black out. Even if I had good directions on where to go, I'd likely get lost. I never have had a good sense of direction." God would forgive him for the lie. He had a keen sense of his location, the way some people had perfect pitch.

"Well, yes, I suppose I will need to accompany you."

"Great. Come inside while I collect my coat."

Gracie hesitated. Hank could almost see the war raging inside of her. After a moment, she stepped into the parsonage. She stood just inside the door, as if she feared the necessity of a quick escape.

Hiding his amusement, Hank reluctantly turned off the television and reached for his thick coat, which he'd tossed across the back of the sofa. His half-eaten peanut-butter-and-jelly sandwich remained on the plate.

"That was your dinner?" Gracie asked.

"Yup. I assumed the church widows would be delivering me casseroles," he teased, and to his amazement, he saw Gracie's lips quiver with what might be construed as a smile. He stared at her for a full minute. "You know, Gracie, you're actually quite lovely."

The frown snapped back into place as fast as an alligator's jaw. "Don't you dare flirt with me, Hank Colfax."

"Oops, sorry." He hid a smile as they left the house together.

His truck was parked out front and he opened the door for her and then placed his hand on her elbow to help her inside. She paused halfway into the vehicle and stared down at him. "You don't need to open the door for me, either. I'm capable of doing that on my own."

"Of course, you are," he said, determined to remain as agreeable as possible.

"It was a nice gesture, though," she conceded.

Hank could have sworn she blushed before she looked away. Once she'd settled inside, he closed her door and then raced around the front of the truck and hopped into the driver's side.

He turned on the ignition and then cranked the heater up as far as it would go. Sleet pelted against the windshield. Snow was forecast for the rest of the week. Winter weather in the northeast corner of Washington State was often brutal.

"You set?" he asked.

"I am. And thank you. I wasn't sure what to expect when I came to the house."

He turned to look at her in the dim light from the street lighting. "I promise to read over the list before bed tonight."

"That will make both our lives much easier."

The truck choked out a plume of black smoke before they drove off. "You comfortable?" he asked.

"Yes, thanks."

They rode in silence to the end of the street before Gracie seemed to relax. The truck's heater made it cozy warm.

"I don't know how this switch between you and Peter is going to work. This is an especially busy week."

"At The Last Call, too," he said, concerned for the first time. Pete's list burned a hole in his pocket. He had no clue what was going to be asked of him over the next week.

"I can't help wondering how Peter is doing."

Hank was thinking the same thing. The poor sucker had no clue what he was getting himself into.

CHAPTER FOUR

"Tilt the glass," the grisly, bearded man sitting on the other side of the bar snapped at Pete. "Look at all the foam that's collecting. Do you even know what you're doing?"

"Sorry," Pete said, and quickly followed the old man's advice. He had an unkempt beard and wore a ratty-looking knit cap with several moth-eaten holes.

"You ain't no bartender," the man sitting next to the bearded one commented, eyeing Pete curiously.

"That I'm not." Pete was in full agreement. Hard as he tried, he couldn't keep up. Hank had mentioned needing to hire extra help, and that was no joke. The tavern was packed, and he was stuck with doing it all. Filling pitchers of beer, delivering them to the tables of demanding clients, collecting the money, washing mugs. He hadn't had a single moment to stop and breathe from the time The Last Call opened.

"Hey, we need another pitcher of beer over here," a rowdy group of lumberjacks shouted from the center of the room.

"On it," Pete promised. He was sweating, and no way was he keeping up with the orders. He needed help and he needed it desperately. Hank had warned him Mondays would be busy because of the football game. Several of the patrons were involved in watching the television and didn't seem to pay attention to how long it took him to refill their beers. The reprieve didn't last long, however. Unrest followed, with irritating shouts from customers wanting refills. Pete was working as fast as he could and didn't have a hope of catching up.

Grabbing another pitcher, Peter started to fill it, slanting it as the old man had advised. It did help, but the foam seemed to accumulate ahead of the liquid. Already there were shouts of discontent rising from the tables.

"Where's Hank?"

Pete looked up from the pitcher. "He's taking a few days off."

The man frowned. "Never said anything about it."

"Yes, well, it was a spur-of-the-moment decision."

"It must have been an emergency for him to get this yahoo to fill in," the grisly man at the bar commented to the one sitting next to him.

"I'm Pete," he said, taking the opportunity to introduce himself to the bar patrons.

"Walt here," the one with the unkempt beard said.

Pete glanced up long enough to grin. "Hank mentioned you. Said you were one of his best customers."

"Did he say anything about me?"

"And you are?"

"Rowdy."

"Yeah," Walt said, "and he earned his name, so you best get that mug of beer to him before he trashes the place."

"I'm working on it," Pete promised, but Rowdy's order was third or fourth down the line. Pete was overwhelmed, and panic was starting to settle in.

After what seemed like a lifetime, the pitcher was filled to the brim. Pete scurried around the bar to deliver it to the table of lumberjacks. They were a motley crew, dressed in overalls and steel-toed boots. Clumps of mud were spread across the wooden floor.

A group of men at the dartboard glared at him and one said, "Isn't that our pitcher? We asked first."

"Sorry, sorry. Coming right up." Pete raced back and grabbed a second pitcher.

"Hey, what about me?" Rowdy asked, sounding un-happy.

In his work as a pastor, the one thing Pete knew how to do was enlist volunteers. "How about you pour your own."

Rowdy's eyes lit up before he hopped down from the barstool and joined Pete on the other side of the bar. "You ain't no good at this, boy."

Rowdy wasn't telling Pete something he didn't already know. "Thanks, I appreciate the help."

"Hey, I'm no barmaid," Rowdy said with a huff. "I'll get my own beer, but I'm not getting anyone else's."

So much for a reprieve or a helping hand.

The football game ended at close to ten o'clock, and thankfully, tabs paid, the tavern settled down to a man-ageable level. Pete remained busy. His heart slowed to a normal rate and some of the more verbal discontent died down as those at the tables slowly headed home.

What surprised Pete was how physically draining this gig had turned out to be. His back ached, his feet hurt. It felt as if he'd put in a full day of baling hay, a job he'd taken after high school to pay for his college expenses. Hardest physical labor he'd ever done. He hadn't antici-pated that tending bar would be equal to that summer's exhausting work.

The roar of motorcycles screaming was loud enough to shake the tavern's windows. Everyone looked up as the clamor suddenly went silent. A few minutes later, the door opened, and six of the biggest tattooed men Pete had ever seen swaggered in through the door as if they owned the place. They wore black leather vests, with chains hanging from their back pockets attached to their wallets.

Walt turned to Rowdy and chuckled. "This should be good."

Pete forced a welcoming smile. The last thing he wanted was to give the impression he was intimidated. He was, but he refused to show it.

Wiping his hands on the white cloth wrapped around his waist, Pete asked, "What can I get you boys?"

"Boys?" the leader of the group asked with a fierce glare. "Do I look like a boy to you?"

"Nope, not at all," Pete said, and while his knees were practically knocking, he didn't let his discomfort show. "A slip of the tongue."

"Don't let it happen again." The threat was there, clear as vodka.

"Sure thing," Pete said, as casually as he could modulate his voice. He leaned forward, and automatically reached for six mugs.

"Where's Hank?"

"Vacationing," Walt supplied. "Hired this yahoo to take his place."

"What's your name?" the biker asked Pete.

"Pete . . . Pete Armstrong."

All six men sat down at the bar and ordered beers. Working as fast as he could, Pete poured beer from the tap, and hoped they didn't notice the way his hand shook as he set the first glass along the top of the bar.

"He ain't much of a bartender," Rowdy informed them, which only added to Pete's discomfort.

"You got that right," biker number two said, staring Pete down.

"What're you riding?" Pete asked, thinking to involve the bikers in friendly conversation. If he could keep them engaged, they might not mind how long it took him to deliver the brews.

"What do you want to know for?"

"Just curious."

"Anyone who knows anything about us knows we ride Harleys."

"Right," Pete said.

"What about you, *boy*? You ride?"

Boy! The challenge was there, one Pete chose to ignore. "Nope, can't say that I do. I've never had the opportunity."

"Like Walt here says, you ain't no bartender."

"No, I'll admit this is my first gig; I'm still learning the ropes. Appreciate the patience." As he spoke, he filled each mug and set them on the counter, avoiding eye contact.

"What do you do?"

"Do?" Pete hesitated. If he admitted he was the pastor at Light of Life church in Bridgeport, he could see the conversation taking a turn in a direction he wanted to avoid. As soon as the patrons learned he was a man of the cloth, everything would change. He'd seen it happen far too often. It was like people put up a wall, blocking him out, as if afraid he would judge them. Then there were the ones who pretended their lives were perfect in every way. They hid behind their righteousness, afraid that if Pete really knew what was going on in their lives he would take it upon himself to preach them into God's kingdom.

"Seeing as you don't usually tend bars, what's your job?"

"Bet he sits behind a desk all day, Pres," one of the bikers said, snickering.

"Looks real soft to me. Probably hasn't done a day's work in his life."

"Baled hay," Pete told them.

"No one's baling hay now."

"True, and admittedly that was a few years back." Pete didn't know why these rough-and-tough men were interested in him. He was happy to serve them beer and make casual conversation. It was as if they were looking for something . . . or someone.

"So, what's up?" he asked, placing the last of the filled mugs on the counter.

"What's up is: You aren't Hank. We're curious why he would choose you. Doesn't look to me like you belong here."

"Actually, I do," he said, remaining as amicable as he could manage, given the circumstances. "Hank asked me to fill in for him while he's . . . away for a few days."

"And I'll ask again, what is it you normally do?"

Pete couldn't understand why they continued to press him on this.

"Answer the question!" The words were sharp and demanding.

"Now, Switchblade, be nice." Snake, the biker with *Pres* on his leather vest, asked. "Maybe he doesn't want to tell us and needs a bit of inducement."

"I'm in human resources," Pete supplied, thinking quickly.

"Human resources?" Snake barked a laugh. "What's that?"

"I help people."

"He does what?" The biggest, burliest of the men leaned across the bar. "What did that mean, Gunner?"

"He helps people," Gunner repeated.

"Actually, it's a bit more than that," Pete said, wanting to clarify himself with a more accurate description. "I also lecture."

"Lecture?"

"La-tee-da," Snake said, with a gruff, sarcastic laugh.

"What do you lecture on?" Gunner asked, cocking his head at an angle. His hair was long and fell to one side as he sized up Pete.

Oh boy, every time he opened his mouth, Pete dug himself deeper into the hole.

"My friend asked you a question." Switchblade slid off the barstool and narrowed his eyes on Pete as he menacingly reached to grab hold of Pete's shirt, hauling him halfway across the bar.

"Settle down," Snake barked, stopping his friend by raising his hand.

Switchblade released Pete, who fell back onto his feet and drew in a shaky breath.

While still posed in a halting position, Snake said, "Pete here is about to tell us how he helps people by giving them lectures."

"It isn't like that, I . . ." Pete paused long enough to swallow. "I'm more of a teacher than someone who gives lectures."

Walt muttered and shook his head. "He looks like some fancy professor with the way he dresses."

Snake ignored Walt's comment. "What do you teach?"

"Yeah, I'd be curious, too," Rowdy said, "because I can tell you've never been to bartending school."

"Can't say that I have," Pete admitted, working hard

at not showing how intimidated he felt. Walt was right. With his button-down shirt and his clean-cut looks, he stuck out like a penguin in a birdcage.

"Seems you have yet to answer the question."

"Okay, since you want to know," he said thinking fast, and remaining as vague as possible, "I teach ancient Middle Eastern literature."

All eight men sitting at the bar looked at him, and then at one another, as if Pete had been speaking Greek.

"You trying to show us up, boy?" Snake demanded, eyes narrowing.

"Of course not. I simply answered your question."

"You think you're smarter than the rest of us?"

"Not at all," Pete insisted.

"He's a real know-it-all," Switchblade chimed in.

Snake slid off the stool and glared at Pete. "You rubbing your education in our faces is an insult to every man here."

"Let me assure you that wasn't my intention." Pete started to backpedal as fast as he could, wondering how this conversation could have disintegrated so quickly.

"It seems to me," Snake said, looking thoughtful, "this here genius needs a lesson in humility."

Walt leaned toward Rowdy. "Told you this was going to be good."

"Yup. I can see it comin'," Walt said, scratching the side of his full beard.

"I'm actually quite humble already," Pete felt the need to say. "Working this bar has kept me that way all night. I'm not exactly cut out for this job, but I'm doing my best."

"Sometimes folks like you need more of an object lesson," Gunner told him.

"Object lesson?" Switchblade repeated. "Hey, Snake, that's a good idea. We can't let no college boy spout off his smarts to us."

Before Pete understood what was happening two of the biggest bikers came around the bar. One stood at each side of him. They grabbed hold by his elbows and lifted his feet several inches off the ground as they effortlessly carried him out from behind the bar.

"Wait," Pete protested, "where are you taking me?" He didn't bother to struggle, knowing it wouldn't do any good. He twisted his head to look at one biker and then the other. Both ignored him as they walked across the room to where the dartboard was pinned to the wall.

"Stand there and don't move," Snake instructed, as he plucked the darts from the board.

"Stand here?" Pete swallowed tightly. "Why?"

Snake ran his fingers over the tips of the darts as though testing their sharpness.

Pete swallowed tightly.

"If you value your more vulnerable body parts, I'd advise you to keep still." Snake raised his arm, took aim, and tossed the dart, which whizzed past Pete's right ear.

Pete gulped.

"That was close," Switchblade said, and slapped Snake across the back. "Let me give it a try."

Pete's mouth had gone dry. He swallowed and resisted the urge to duck as Switchblade took over Snake's spot.

Pete squeezed his eyes closed.

The tavern door opened. Pete squinted through his closed eyes and noticed it was a woman. One he knew. One he'd seen that very day.

She seemed to quickly assess the situation. "What's going on here?" she demanded. "Snake, what are you doing?!"

"Ah, come on, Bambi, we're just having a little fun."

They were shocked by her audacity as she moved to block Pete from their view. "A little fun?" she repeated. "Come on, guys, enough is enough."

Pete's eyes flew open, and sure enough it was the very waitress who had served him and Hank lunch that afternoon. The one who had attracted his attention and whom he'd thought about during the entire drive back to Bridgeport. They called her Bambi, but the name tag she wore at Mom's Place said her name was Millie. He couldn't imagine what she was doing here and was mortified that she would be the one to come to his rescue.

———

Millie served drinks, which was how she knew the bikers who called themselves Hell's Outlaws. Millie liked them because they were generous tippers, whereas the majority of customers were inclined to leave her a dime, if that. She might have gotten bigger tips if she'd been willing to show a bit more of her body, which was something Millie refused to do. Working in a strip club was humiliating enough. She hated the job, hated the name the strip club had assigned her, but none of the girls, onstage or off, used their real names. Still, she needed the money if she was going to make rent. That and what she made working the lunch shift at Mom's Place was just enough to get her by, month to month, with no extras. Because she didn't drive, she spent a good portion of her pay on taxi rides.

"Never thought you'd be a killjoy," Snake muttered, as he set aside the darts.

For that matter, neither did Millie. If it was anyone else, she might have turned a blind eye. But it was him. The man whose smile she hadn't been able to forget all afternoon.

CHAPTER FIVE

Present Day

"Nana, this is a really good story."

Nana thought it was the best story ever, although she didn't say so.

"I like the bikers best," Lance said. "Grandpa has a bike, and he sometimes takes me on rides."

Nana hid a grin. Lance's grandpa loved his Harley almost as much as he loved his family. It was his most prized possession.

"I like that Millie saved Pete. Girl power." Lily thrust her small fist into the air.

"Did she change her name to Millie because she didn't like the name her mama gave her? Alice in my class changed her name; she asked people to call her Peach. That's a silly name."

"Millie changed her name because she didn't want people to know her real name because of where she worked."

Lance cocked his head to one side. "What kind of job was that?"

No use scooting around the facts. "Millie worked as a server at a . . . dance club in Kettle Springs."

"You mean like a strip club?" Lance asked.

"Well . . . yes."

"A strip club?" Lily asked.

"It's where women undress for men," Lance explained.

How her grandson knew this, Nana didn't want to know.

Lily's eyes grew as big as fried eggs. "Is that right, Nana?"

"It is."

Lily let out a deep sigh. "Poor Millie."

"That's how the bikers knew her," Lance explained to his sister, as if he was a man of the world. "Isn't that right, Nana?"

"Yup, that's where they knew our Millie."

"Are you ready to get back to the story?" Nana asked, eager to change the subject.

"Not yet," Lance said. "I want to know why the bikers kept quizzing Pete about his job."

Nana sighed, anxious to avoid the subject. "That's another story, but the short version is that the Hell's Outlaws were on the lookout for someone who was dealing drugs in town. Rumor had it that the guy responsible was someone they wouldn't normally suspect."

"And they thought it was Pete?" Lance asked. "The pastor?"

"They did, and when he hesitated and didn't give them an up-front answer, they were convinced it must be him."

"Did they ever find the drug dealer?"

"That's not really part of our story."

"I want to know about the bikers and the drug dealer," Lance insisted.

"It might ruin the story about Pete and Hank," Nana warned.

"Don't tell us, don't tell us," Lily cried, covering her ears with both hands while burrowing her face against Nana's side.

"Tell us," Lance insisted, ignoring his younger sister.

"Okay, if you must know," Nana lowered her voice to a whisper. "By Christmas, the bikers had a change of heart."

"What does that mean?" Lance cocked his head to one side, as if his nana had spoken a foreign language.

Nana slowly shook her head. "You'll have to wait until the end of the story. I promise it will be worth it once you hear what happens to Snake and the rest of Hell's Outlaws."

"Rowdy and Walt?"

"Them, too."

Lily roused herself. "I have a question. What about Gracie and Hank? Did they get Hortense, the mule?"

Nana hung her head in order to hide her amusement. "I was just about to pick up the story there."

"They aren't going to kiss, are they?" Lance grumbled. "Because if they do, I need to know ahead of time so I can plug my ears."

"I'll give you fair warning," Nana promised, as she returned to the story.

CHAPTER SIX

"Are you warm enough?" Hank asked Gracie. The heater in the old Ford truck was temperamental at best. It'd blast out heat and then for no rhyme or reason would change to frigid cold air.

"It's fine."

Hank glanced at the woman sitting next to him. She had her arms crossed and glared straight ahead. "You don't seem happy," he commented.

"I'm happy."

"That's not what the look you're wearing says."

"Okay, if you must know, I'd much rather be sitting in front of my fireplace reading a good book. Monday night is all about football, and I can't stand the game."

Hank suspected Gracie frowned upon just about anything that could be construed as fun. He wondered how it was that Pete's sister could be so vastly different from her brother.

"What happened to you, Gracie?" he asked, before he could stop himself.

"What do you mean?" she snapped, turning her head enough to glare at him.

"The girl I remember in high school—"

"I'm not that girl," she said, cutting him off.

"I know. You used to laugh—"

"I laugh." She gathered her coat more tightly around herself, effectively conveying the message: Anything from her past was a closed subject.

Hank feared he'd wandered into mine-infested territory and considered it best to change the subject. "Sorry, I didn't mean to pry."

"I have a good life," she insisted, as if she needed to prove it to herself. "A very good life. I work for the church and head the Ladies Missionary Society, I play the piano for the church, and give lessons. My life is full."

"What about men?" he dared to ask.

"I certainly don't need a man in my life."

"I didn't mean to imply that you did. Are you dating anyone special?"

"I . . . no, not at the moment. Why all these questions? Why do you care if I'm dating or not?"

Hank didn't have an answer. He didn't know why he was interested and hated that he was. "Just curious," he said with a shrug, dismissing his interest.

Gracie gave him the silent treatment until after they'd collected the horse trailer. "Pay attention here. Farmer Martin's place is the second mailbox past the giant fir tree in the next bend."

"Got it."

"It's easy to miss, and you aren't going to want to have to turn around when you're hauling this trailer."

"Right. I'll keep my eyes peeled." He looked over and smiled at her.

"Kindly pay attention to the road."

"I am."

"No, you're not, you keep looking at me."

"I can't help it. I forgot how pretty you are," he teased. He knew this was the last thing Gracie wanted to hear and loved getting a reaction out of her.

"What did I say about you flirting with me?" she demanded.

"I wasn't flirting," he insisted. Suppressing a smile was almost impossible. He loved the way she took everything so seriously, because it made it easy to get a rise out of her. His comments clearly flustered her. He enjoyed the way her cheeks flushed a fetching shade of pink, and because of that he couldn't make himself stop.

"You're going to miss the turn," she cried, and reached out to hold on to the dashboard as if he was about to slam on his brakes.

He eased his foot off the accelerator and made the turn as smooth as Mario Andretti at the last Indy 500. Hank pulled into the yard and parked the truck with an expert hand, as if he often drove hauling a horse trailer. He leaped out of the driver's seat and went around to help Gracie out of the passenger side. She didn't complain this time when he offered her a hand, although she didn't take it.

Farmer Martin must have seen their headlights because the porch screen door slammed closed as he walked down the steps to greet them.

"I wasn't sure you were going to make it," he said. "Looks like there's a snowstorm headed our way."

"A promise is a promise."

The old man, dressed in coveralls, a thick coat, and a trapper hat with fur-lined ear flaps, steered them toward the barn. "Hortense is a stubborn one, so you best let me lead her into the trailer."

"Have at it," Hank said gratefully.

"You should know this mule has got a mind of her own."

Hank was tempted to claim Gracie shared Hortense's temperament, but resisted, which probably spared him a good tongue-lashing. He'd never met a woman like Gracie, and as much as he hated to admit it, he yearned to break through that concrete wall she'd built around herself. From the evidence thus far, it seemed to rival the Great Wall of China. She hadn't answered him when he asked what had happened that caused her to close herself off from men. But Hank was determined to find out what made Gracie tick. Perhaps at the end of the week, he'd ask Pete, although Hank had the feeling even her brother wasn't completely in the know.

The farmer looked Hank up and down. "Ralph Martin," he said, and held out his hand.

"Hank Colfax." The two exchanged handshakes.

"You Grace Ann's man?"

"He most certainly is not," Gracie blurted out, as though that was the most ridiculous thing she'd ever heard. "Hank is . . . He's sort of helping Peter this week. We are not romantically involved in any way whatsoever."

Ralph held Hank's gaze, lowered his voice, and muttered, "That's a shame."

Hank chuckled.

"Let's get Hortense in that trailer," Ralph said, leading the way across the yard.

Hank followed Ralph Martin into the barn, thinking it might be a good idea to introduce himself to Hortense before getting her into the trailer. He walked over to the horse stall where the mule stood. Hortense eyed him with suspicion.

"Hello, Hortense," he said, and reached out to pet her nose.

"I wouldn't—"

Before Hank could draw his hand back, Hortense bit him.

"Told you she isn't the friendliest of beasts," Farmer Martin reminded him.

Luckily it was more of a nip than a real bite. Hank jerked his hand back and shook it several times to dispel the pain. "She reminds me of someone else I know."

Ralph chuckled. "Don't need to tell me who, do you?"

"Nope," Hank said, as the two shared a smile.

They loaded Hortense into the trailer, and before long, Gracie and Hank, along with Hortense, were heading back into town.

They'd gone only a short way when, just as he'd feared, the heat made an automatic switch to cold air.

"Turn it off," Gracie insisted, shivering in the icy-cold explosion of air.

Hank hurriedly flipped the switch to the off position.

"Are you trying to freeze me to death?" she demanded.

"No, why would I do that? This is an old truck. Hauling this trailer is taking everything ole Marilyn has got."

"Marilyn."

"Named her Marilyn, after Marilyn McCoo from the 5th Dimension."

"The 5th what?"

"Don't you ever listen to the radio?" This woman had her head buried so deep in the sand she was looking at the Eiffel Tower.

"As a matter of fact, I don't appreciate modern music. I prefer listening to hymns. I swear the lyrics from popular songs come directly from the mouth of Satan."

Hank bit his tongue to keep from commenting. He should have expected as much. What was that saying about Gracie? Ah, he remembered. She was so heavenly minded, she was no earthly good. Yup, that was Pete's sister.

"You do realize it's ridiculous to give inanimate objects names," Gracie seemed to feel obliged to tell him.

"If you say so," he returned, refusing to argue with her.

He was willing to admit how cold it was. His bones were freezing. It was a good thing that he'd dressed for the weather with a winter coat, gloves, and a scarf. Gracie had, too. Winters in this half of the state could be brutal.

He was chilled to his very core, and he knew Gracie must be, too. She rubbed her folded arms a few times as if to get the blood flowing.

"It shouldn't be much longer now before you're home and warm again," he said, encouraging her.

"I know. You must be cold, too."

"I am, but if you'd be willing, I think a few kisses would warm me up."

"Stop it," she snapped, and slugged his arm.

Hank laughed. "Thought that would get a rise out of you."

It'd started to snow, and with the wind, it looked like they might be in for a December blizzard. Hank didn't relish the thought of turning back around and delivering the horse trailer to the Carneys.

As they neared the church, Gracie seemed to relax. She explained that the animals for the Nativity were being kept in an old garage that was behind the parsonage. It was unfortunate that they had to collect Hortense this early, but as she explained earlier, there was no help for it. It was now or the live Nativity on Christmas Eve would go without a mule.

"As part of my duties, will I be required to feed Hortense until Saturday?" Hank asked.

"You'd know the answer if you'd read the list I made for you."

"Seeing that I haven't, as you so kindly reminded me, perhaps you could update me."

She sent him a prissy look and said, "Ken Lambert is seeing to that."

"Ken Lambert," Hank repeated. The picture of his

former classmate instantly came to mind. Ken ran cross-country with them and, if he remembered correctly, went into the service after graduation. He seemed to remember that Ken and Gracie had once been an item. "How's Ken doing these days?"

"He's good. Married a girl from Vietnam and they have a couple kids."

Her toneless response caught his attention. "Didn't you date Ken at one point?"

"Years ago," she said, as if that, too, was a closed subject. Then, because she felt she needed Hank to know, she added, "We were never really anything more than . . . friends."

Interesting. Hank wanted to press her for more. The temptation was strong, but he had the feeling Gracie would close up tighter than Fort Knox if he asked for details. Ken was definitely someone she didn't want to discuss. If he got any information about the relationship between Ken and Gracie it would need to come from Pete. He made a mental note to ask his friend when they next met.

Getting Hortense out of the trailer didn't prove to be as much of a problem as Hank had anticipated. He got a carrot from the house, and Hortense followed him as calm as could be.

The sheep were already in the garage, and they eyed

Hortense with interest. Before he left to return the horse trailer, he made sure the animals were warm and had enough feed and water until morning.

"I'll drive you home," he offered Gracie, unwilling for her to walk back in the middle of a snowstorm.

"That would be appreciated."

"Gracie, come on, did you really think I'd leave you to walk alone in the dark in a snowstorm?"

"How many times do I need to remind you my name is Grace Ann?"

"You'll always be Gracie to me."

Her pinched lips told him what she thought of his ignoring her request. Hank wasn't concerned. Given time, she'd get used to it.

He held the truck door open for her. She frowned at him, as if to remind him, once again, she was fully capable of opening her own door. To her credit, she let it pass without comment.

The heater was back on, and once it warmed the air, they both reveled in the blast of heat.

"That hot air feels good."

"It does," he agreed.

Her small rented duplex was only a few blocks from the church. When he parked at the curb, Gracie turned to look at him. "If you need me to ride with you to return the trailer, I will."

Hank was pleasantly surprised by her offer. "I'll be fine."

The relief showed in her expression.

"Thanks anyway." He started to get out of the truck, but she stopped him by placing her hand on his forearm.

"I'm good. Enjoy the rest of your evening, Hank."

"I appreciate all your help with this," he told her, and waited until she was safely inside the house with her light on before he drove off.

Forty minutes later he was back in Bridgeport, taking time to appreciate the Christmas lights that decorated Main Street and all the local shops. He returned in time for the sports update on the late news to learn the 49ers had lost to the Dallas Cowboys. He wished he'd been able to watch the game in its entirety. Then again, he'd spent the time with Gracie and come to know her a bit more. It'd been a fair trade-off. She was a hard nut to crack, but that didn't dissuade him. Before the end of the week, he was determined to discover the woman behind that protective wall.

After a long, hot shower, he headed to bed and was asleep within minutes.

The phone woke him. Rolling over, he looked at the clock on the bedstand.

One-thirty-six.

Another emergency? Tossing aside the covers, he stumbled into the kitchen, where the wall phone was mounted.

"This better be good," he muttered, as he grabbed hold of the receiver.

"It's Ken Lambert. Where's Pastor Armstrong?"

"Away. I'm taking his place. It's Hank. Hank Colfax."

The hesitation from Ken told him he was curious as to why Hank was answering Pete's phone. He resisted, though.

"You looked out the window lately?"

"Nope. I was in bed, sound asleep. You should be, too."

"I'm a deputy these days, in case you didn't know."

Hank didn't.

"You got a problem, Hank. There's a mule loose on Main Street, and I suspect it's the one I saw you driving into town with a few hours ago."

CHAPTER SEVEN

The conversation taking place between the waitress he knew as Millie from Mom's Place and the bikers confused Pete. On the plus side, he was no longer forced to be the target for their dart practice, which to his way of thinking was good news. Millie or Bambi, whichever her name was, pulled the bikers aside. Pete could hear only bits and pieces of the conversation. She seemed to be assuring the men Pete wasn't the person they sought.

"He says he lectures people," Snake said, with a fierce look that pinned Pete to the wall as keenly as one of those darts might have done.

"Perhaps I can help," Pete offered, striding over to where the bikers had gathered. They'd formed a circle around the woman. He tried to get their attention, to no avail, and raised his finger to interrupt their conversation. "Excuse me, if I could say a word here, we could clear up whatever is the trouble."

He was ignored and finally accepted none of those involved were interested in what he had to say.

Millie/Bambi looked uncomfortable, but to her credit, she held her own. Pete caught her tossing him a pleading look that he wasn't able to read. With bulging muscles and heavily tattooed arms, the bikers would have intimidated Bruce Lee, and Pete was no exception. But he needed to do something.

"What seems to be the problem here?" he said, in his most demanding voice. As he spoke, he edged his way between the ones called Switchblade and Gunner. Both stood with their feet braced apart. Pete might as well have been trying to move the Berlin Wall, for all the progress he made.

"Snake thinks you might be cutting into his business," Millie/Bambi explained.

"What's his business, because I'm fairly certain—"

"Not your concern," Gunner interrupted, then lifted Pete by the scruff of his neck and easily set him aside.

Several moments passed before the bikers broke rank and, after grumbling among themselves, left the tavern. Walt and Rowdy remained sitting at the bar, although they'd swiveled around for a bird's-eye view of the confrontation. They both looked enormously amused by Pete's predicament.

Pete returned to the bar and noticed the two regulars grinning like they held winning pull-tab tickets.

"You're a good sport," Rowdy commented, as Pete re-filled his mug with frothy beer.

"Watching you with those bikers was the best fun I've had in a month of Sundays," Walt added, and slapped his hand against the top of the bar as he released what might have been a laugh, albeit rusty.

"Happy to entertain you both," Pete muttered. He wondered how Hank would have managed the situation, and was convinced he would consider it all in a night's work.

Millie/Bambi slowly approached the bar. Pete was mortified that she'd been the one to rescue him, and at the same time he was blissfully grateful. He felt awkward and uncomfortable, and hadn't a clue who they thought he was or what business of theirs he'd undermined.

"Guess I owe you my thanks."

She shrugged away his appreciation. "You should know my name isn't really Bambi. It's Millie. Just plain Millie."

"The truth is, I don't know what I said that set them off—"

"It wasn't you," she said, cutting him off. "They're

looking for someone and seemed to think you fit the bill."

Remembering how he'd hedged the biker's questions, Pete had to admit his vague answers probably raised their suspicions.

"You seemed to know them," he commented, and assumed they must frequent Mom's Place the same way he and Hank did.

Millie lowered her head, avoiding eye contact. "I know them from Toy's Dancers."

The strip club in the seedy part of Kettle Springs was notorious. It catered to truckers and lowlifes. It wasn't someplace he would think a beautiful woman like Millie would frequent, unless . . . Pete didn't like the place his mind went to. Millie up onstage dancing for those men.

"You work at Toy's?" Pete asked, before he could stop himself.

"I waitress there in the evenings."

"Oh." So Millie wasn't one of the girls who seductively removed her clothes. That small detail comforted him, although he hated the thought of her in that toxic environment.

"I hate it," she admitted, "but it was the only job I could find in the evenings. Working part-time at Mom's Place doesn't give me enough money to pay rent, and the electric bill, let alone put food on the table."

"I imagine it doesn't. How can I help?"

Her head shot up as if that was the last thing she expected to hear. "You could give me a job here," she rushed to say, her words full of nervous energy. "I'm a hard worker and I'm fine with whatever you can pay me, as long as I can keep my tips. I can do this job, no problem."

Pete didn't know how to respond. It wasn't his place to hire anyone without Hank's approval. Refusing her after all she'd done to save him weighed heavily on him. He owed Millie.

"He can certainly use the help," Walt inserted.

"One thing for sure, he doesn't have a clue on how to pour beer. Got more head than brew. Maybe you could teach Pete a few things."

Millie held Pete's gaze, and it seemed she was holding her breath at the same time.

"I'll need to check with Hank," he said.

Millie's eyes fell and she nodded. "Before you do, you should probably know I got fired from Toy's." She bit into her lower lip. "One of the customers assumed . . . you know . . . He seemed to think I was something I'm not, and when he got overly . . . friendly, I slapped him."

Pete could imagine the management didn't take kindly to having their clientele abused.

"All I do is serve drinks, and I don't want there to be any misunderstanding as to anything else."

"No misunderstanding here," Pete assured her.

"Not at The Last Call, or Toy's, or anyplace else, for that matter," she said, her lower lip trembling.

"I'll make sure that's clear. If any of the customers here think otherwise, I'll set them straight."

Her head shot up. "You mean I have the job?" she asked, and then immediately added, "You won't be sorry, I promise."

"For now, yes, but I'll need to clear this with Hank." Pete remembered what his friend told him over lunch: Hank seemed to have trouble finding good help. Heaven knew Pete had failed miserably at bartending. The few instructions Hank had tossed on his way out the door had done little to prepare him. He felt like a fish in a mud-hole, desperately struggling to find water.

"Thank you," Millie said, her deep blue eyes revealing her gratitude. Right away she grabbed a tray and started clearing off the tables. Pete had been so busy he hadn't gotten around to it after the football game ended.

As soon as she had cleared and wiped down the tables, she washed and replaced the mugs. She seemed to want to prove to Pete that he hadn't made a mistake hiring her. He could only speculate how Hank would react when he learned Pete had hired a waitress.

The Last Call didn't close until midnight on weekdays and two on the weekends. By eleven-thirty, Pete was dragging. Mondays were technically his day off, although time away from his duties as a pastor wasn't dictated by a day of the week. It was a rare day he had to himself.

With Millie's help, all the mugs were washed and placed back on the shelf. The floors were swept, and the tables cleaned, with chairs hoisted upside down on the tabletops. If Pete had tackled the task on his own, he suspected it would have taken twice as long.

He placed the *closed* sign in the window and was more than ready to call it a night. And what a night it had been. Four more to go.

"I'll walk you to your car," Pete offered, wanting to be sure Millie got home safely.

"I . . . don't have a car."

Stunned, Pete asked, "How did you get from Toy's to here?"

"I walked. It's only a couple miles and I thought . . . I hoped Hank would take pity on me and give me a job. I wasn't expecting to find you here."

"Hank and I have been friends since our school days."

"I've seen you at Mom's Place a number of times."

"We make sure we get together at least once a month, and on rare occasions twice if we can manage it."

"It must be wonderful to have such a close friend. Is Hank all right? I mean, he's usually here."

"We decided to trade places this week."

"Right before Christmas?"

"So it seems," Pete said, wondering how Hank was getting along. One thing was certain, his friend had gotten the better end of this deal. Pete's feet ached and he had a cramp in his back from standing for the last ten hours.

"I know Hank owns this tavern, but what is it you do?"

Remembering the trouble he'd gotten himself into by not giving a direct answer to the bikers, Pete decided to be upfront with Millie. "I'm the pastor for Light of Life church in Bridgeport."

Millie's mouth dropped as she stared at him, as if seeing him for the first time.

"I'd appreciate it if you didn't let the word out while I'm here in Hank's stead."

"Okay." She stepped back from him as if she expected him to grab hold and force her to be baptized.

"Millie," he said, softening his voice. "I'm not going to judge you for working at Toy's or for anything else. That's not my way, and it's not God's way, either. We all do what is necessary to make it in this life."

"Thank you," she whispered. "If you don't mind, I'd like to use the phone."

"Of course." Although Pete couldn't imagine who Millie would be calling at this late hour. When he heard her order a taxi, he interrupted her: "Millie, wait."

Holding her hand over the mouthpiece, she looked expectantly to him, her beautiful blue eyes full of question.

"I'll drive you to wherever you need to go."

"You don't need to do that. It's late and you must be tired."

It was and he was. Nevertheless, he realized Millie needed every penny she earned. "I'm happy to do it." And that was as true as her objections.

She canceled the ride and thanked him again.

"Come on, let's get you home." He reached for his coat and grabbed his car keys.

When they stepped outside, Pete found the snow was falling in blizzardlike conditions. He knew Millie must have been chilled to the bone in her walk from the strip club to The Last Call. Her coat was thin at best, more suitable for springtime. It didn't escape his notice that when she pulled on her gloves, there were more than a few holes in the knitted fingers.

After he helped her into the passenger seat, he climbed inside and started the engine, revving up the heat. The windshield wipers swished back and forth to clear away the accumulated snow. Soon they were able to look out into the night.

"Do you have family in the area?" he asked.

"Yes," Millie whispered, and tucked her hands between her knees, as if the chill had gotten to her. "Only they want nothing more to do with me."

Pete hardly knew what to say. He couldn't imagine anything Millie could have done that would turn her family against her.

"I got pregnant when I was eighteen," she added, her voice so low that Pete had trouble hearing her.

"You have a baby, then?"

She shook her head. "I miscarried in my third month, but by then my mother made it clear that I wasn't welcome to come back."

"You've been on your own since you were eighteen?"

She nodded.

"What about the baby's father?"

She snickered softly. "He was a college boy, and as soon as I told him I was pregnant, he was gone. He couldn't get away from me fast enough."

"I'm sorry, Millie. You deserve better."

"That's life, right? Live and learn. Well, I learned that lesson quick, and there won't be a repeat."

Other than giving him directions to her rental, they rode in silence down the deserted street on the poor side of town. "That's it over there," she said, pointing to a run-down duplex only a few scant blocks from Toy's. Thank you for the ride."

"You're welcome, Millie."

With her hand on the door handle, she looked back. "What time would you like me to arrive tomorrow?"

"When do you finish at Mom's Place?"

"Usually around two or three. I only work the lunch hour."

"You can come whenever you wish," he said. "I'll connect with Hank and clear the job with him."

"Do you think he'll keep me on?" Her eyes were as hopeful as her voice.

"I can't say." Pete was determined to do his best to make sure she kept the job.

"That's all I can ask." Still, she remained in the car as if there was something more she needed to say. "I hope you don't think poorly of me."

"Millie, please look at me."

She turned back, but avoided making eye contact.

"I'm not here to judge you or anyone," he assured her. "To me, you're a good person, who's working hard to improve her situation. I admire that and will do whatever I can to help."

Sudden tears filled her eyes. Millie blinked them back and whispered, "Thank you, Pastor."

"Pete. I'm Pete. I'll look forward to seeing you again tomorrow afternoon," he said, as she started to exit the car.

He waited as she walked through the snow to her

apartment and realized how much he wanted to know Millie better and was grateful for the opportunity. He'd noticed her long before now, and while he wouldn't admit it to Hank, she was the reason he suggested they meet at Mom's Place for lunch.

CHAPTER EIGHT

It felt like Hank had barely closed his eyes, after his long night of chasing down that stubborn mule, when the alarm next to his bed let out a shrill blast. He sat straight up in bed. Blindly he reached for the clock, intent on turning it off and returning to the warmth and comfort, when he remembered he still hadn't read Gracie's list. Heaven forbid he miss another vital appointment.

With his eyes burning, he grabbed his pants from the floor next to the bed and searched for the list. After emptying every pocket, he discovered that he'd somehow lost it. Where in the name of all that was holy had he put that blasted list? He could only imagine Gracie's ire, should he confess he'd misplaced her precious list.

Thinking about Gracie, Hank couldn't hold back a

smile. Something deep inside him he couldn't name yearned to break through that barrier around her heart. He'd forgotten how lovely she was, despite her efforts to downplay her attractiveness. He wondered what it would be like to kiss her and grinned at the thought, imagining that going one of two ways. She would either melt in his arms, which was probably wishful thinking, or, most likely, she'd slap him silly.

After a cup of coffee and a hot shower, Hank felt better prepared to meet the day. He noticed the lights were on in the church office, which was attached to the church itself. This meant Gracie was already busy at work. With renewed energy, he headed out the door, covering the short space between the parsonage and the church.

"Good morning, Gracie," he greeted, coming in from the cold. The snow accumulation was three or four inches, and with the temperature drop, ice crystals had formed a crust over the top layer.

Gracie glanced up from the typewriter. "Good, you're early. The shovel is stored on the back porch."

"Shovel?"

"Why, yes, you'll need to remove the snow from the walkway. The salt is with the shovel."

The last thing he wanted was to return outside and work. Surely, she was kidding. Her look assured him this was no joke as she pointed him toward the back room.

"It's unlikely anyone will come to the church in this weather," he said, seeking a reprieve.

Gracie glared at him. It was either shovel the snow off the walkway or suffer a tongue-lashing from Pete's sister. "All right, all right," he muttered.

"Thank you," she said, ever so sweetly.

Hank had the feeling she relished the idea of sending him into the cold. "Just remember if I come down with pneumonia, you're going to need to nurse me back to health."

"Would you stop?" she demanded, but Hank saw the smile that tempted the edges of her mouth.

It took the better part of an hour to clear the walkway. At the tavern, he never bothered shoveling snow from the parking lot. Because of all the lifting of the beer kegs, hauling them up from the basement, Hank felt he was in good physical shape. However, lifting a few beer kegs wasn't the same as dealing with snow. By the time he finished, the muscles in his arms and back ached like he'd put in a twelve-hour shift at the tavern.

Once he'd finished and stomped the snow off his boots, he returned to the office. Gracie glanced up and seemed surprised. "Finished, already?"

"Yup. What's on the agenda for today?"

"It's on the list."

"Yes, well . . ."

She frowned. "You lost it, didn't you?"

"Misplaced it. No doubt it will show up soon." He was in no mood for a lecture. "Spare me the sermon, and just tell me what I need to do."

With a huff and a sigh that spoke far more eloquently than any disparaging comments, Gracie reached for the appointment calendar on the side of her desk. "Peter visits Mrs. Millstone every week. She . . . needs attention and special handling."

"Ethel Millstone?"

"You know her?"

"She was Pete's and my fifth-grade teacher. That old biddy is still alive?"

"So it would seem." Gracie's eyes narrowed. "Hank, this is serious. Mrs. Millstone has been a generous donor to the work of the church. You simply can't do or say anything to upset her. She's promised a hefty contribution toward replacing the church roof, and we can't risk offending her."

"Me, say anything inappropriate?" He placed his hand over his heart, as if to suggest the accusation had deeply offended him. "I'll be the picture of diplomacy."

"Please. The church badly needs that roof."

"I promise I won't say anything to upset the old woman. She must be close to eighty."

"Just hold your tongue. She's . . . fragile," she said, as if seeking the right word to describe the old woman.

Seeing it was a bit early for visitation, and he hadn't eaten breakfast, Hank returned to the parsonage. He figured he'd leave around ten. He wouldn't stay long, just enough to satisfy the widow's need to be acknowledged and appreciated for her generosity.

Before he left, he returned to the church office to tell Gracie he was off. "I'll be leaving now."

Gracie stood from behind her desk, her hands clenched together. "Hank, I'm serious, please make nice with Mrs. Millstone, I beg of you."

"I understand. Don't you worry your pretty little head, I'll be gracious as the day is long."

"She'll serve you tea and cookies," Gracie added. "Peter says they're often burned and taste terrible, but whatever you do, don't complain. Eat the cookies and compliment her."

"You want me to lie?"

"Not lie, just don't spit out the cookies, okay, even if they're the worst thing you've ever tasted."

"I'm taking one for the church," Hank promised dramatically.

Sighing with what he could interpret only as gratitude, Gracie sent him off.

By the time he arrived at the Millstone residence, Hank had given himself a good, long pep talk. From what he remembered of his former teacher, she went through life as if sucking on lemons. He'd suffered her ruler across his hands more times than he could count.

He stood on the front porch, gathering his resolve, then rang the doorbell. It took a couple minutes before she answered, as if doing so had burdened her soul. When she saw Hank, any warmth in her greeting quickly evaporated.

"What do you want?" she demanded, in that prim-and-proper tone he recalled from the fifth grade.

"I'm here in Pete's place. Gracie . . . Grace Ann asked me to stop by."

"Where's Pastor Armstrong?"

"Out of town. Sorry, guess I'll have to do."

Snorting her displeasure, she stepped aside, and Hank entered the house, which was unusually cold. "Is there something wrong with your furnace?" he asked. The woman must be close to freezing.

"Oil costs money."

A penny-pincher. This news didn't bode well for a comfortable visit. Nevertheless, Hank was determined to be pleasant.

She turned around to stare at him. "You need a haircut."

"So I've been told."

"Then do something about it. You look like you came from the garbage dump, dressed in rags." She pinched her lips to show her displeasure.

"I'll see to it right away."

This seemed to appease her for the moment, and Hank breathed a sigh of relief.

Following her into the main part of the house, Hank placed his hands in his pockets and tried to start their conversation on a pleasant note. "You have a lovely home," he said, looking around appreciatively. Outside of school, he didn't know much about Ethel Millstone. It appeared her husband had done well for himself as the local bank president.

Mrs. Millstone narrowed her eyes and glared at him. "Are you casing my house, young man? Don't think you'll get away with it. I know all about you and that tavern of yours. You were a troublemaker as a fifth-grader. A leopard doesn't change its spots."

This was interesting; he could only speculate what she'd heard about him. "No worries, Mrs. Millstone, I wouldn't dare."

"Good," she muttered with a firm shake of her head. "Then we understand each other."

"We do." He didn't wait for an invitation, claiming a chair to the left of the old woman. A table rested between the two chairs and held a plate of cookies and two teacups. The cookies looked dreadful, and he grimaced knowing he would soon be offered one. Afraid he'd given himself away, he turned his attention back to her.

"Now tell me why you're here instead of Pastor Armstrong," Mrs. Millstone said, sounding none too pleased.

"I thought I explained; Pete's out of town."

She pinched her lips and narrowed her eyes at Hank. "When you see Pastor Armstrong, tell him I consider it an insult that he'd send you for our regular visitation."

Hank let the comment slide. Instead, he focused his gaze on a table by the fireplace mantel, where a small framed high school graduation picture of a young girl rested. She had the same eyes as the old woman and was a beauty. Hank didn't recall if Mrs. Millstone had children.

"Is that your daughter?" he asked, inclining his head toward the photo.

Ethel paused as she filled his teacup with the weak liquid. "That's none of your business."

"Your niece, then?"

The old woman sighed. "If you must know, apparently that is my granddaughter."

Apparently? "She's beautiful."

"And as stubborn as her father, much to their detriment."

"How so?" As soon as the words left his mouth, Hank knew it was the wrong question to ask.

Ethel Millstone set the teapot aside and settled her back against the chair. She glanced at the photo and shook her head. The pinched, angry look returned. "William and I had only the one son. Billy meant the world to us both. We raised him right, gave him the best education, the best schools, the best of everything. We should have known better than to spoil him. The minute we met the woman he said he'd fallen in love with, we knew she was a gold digger. She came from a broken family and didn't have a penny to her name. She was completely unsuitable for our son. Both William and I suspected she was after our son's inheritance. We forbade the marriage. Billy defied us and married her anyway. What he did was unforgiveable."

"Did the marriage last?"

Mrs. Millstone stiffened. "I wouldn't know. I haven't talked to Billy since that day. Denise, my granddaughter, mailed me that photo. I meant to throw it away but hadn't gotten around to it."

Hank twisted around in his chair. "You mean to say you have turned against your only son and his family?"

Her jaw clenched so hard he wondered if she would break off one of her molars. "As I said, this is none of your affair. Kindly keep your thoughts to yourself, because I have no desire to hear them."

"What about Christmas?"

"What about it?" she demanded.

"You're going to remain in this cold house alone when you could be with your son and his family. What about love and goodwill toward men? Your granddaughter sent you that photo to build the bridge between you and her father. To try to build a relationship with her grandmother."

She stiffened her shoulders and refused to look his way. "They're after my money and I refuse to leave them a penny."

Hank leaped from the chair. "Have they ever asked for help?"

"My son knows better than to try."

Hank shook his head. "Mrs. Millstone, I hardly know what to say."

She glared at him with a laser focus that burned with anger. "I believe it's time you left."

"No, I believe it's time you owned up to who you are." He shook his head, knowing what came next would probably cost the church that roof. His blood was hot, but despite the risk, he couldn't remain quiet.

"Where's your Christmas spirit?" he asked.

"I . . . I—"

"No tree, no wreath, no lights, no warmth. You were a good teacher. It saddens me to see what you've become. You're a bitter, cranky old lady afraid of her own shadow. I don't see the love of God in you, and that is a shame."

"So says the drunkard who works in a tavern."

Hank let the comment slide off his back like rainwater off a leaking church roof.

"I've asked you to leave. I refuse to be insulted in my own home. Now go, and you can tell that church they can forget any further donations from me. I am withdrawing my membership; they'll get nothing more from me."

Hank sadly shook his head. "Hold on to your money, Mrs. Millstone. The church doesn't need it and neither does your son and his family. I hope it makes you happy as you cling to it while you're alone in this beautiful house. I believe you'll find it cold comfort."

"Don't let the door hit you on your way out." With a trembling hand, she pointed the way.

Hank knew there was no going back. "I feel sorry for you. You've turned your back on what is most precious. Love and family. Merry Christmas, Mrs. Millstone, although I sincerely doubt it will be."

He left, standing briefly on the front porch, as he mulled over how terribly wrong this visit had gone. Gracie would never forgive him. He needed to talk to Pete and explain.

Instead of heading back to the church office, he returned to the parsonage and called Pete. His friend answered on the third ring.

"It's Hank," he said after Pete's greeting. "We need to talk."

"Hey, listen, I'm glad you called, I have something to tell you."

"I have something to tell you, too." Wanting to get the bad news out of the way, he added, "Let me go first. I had a run-in with Mrs. Millstone, and it didn't go well." Hank relayed the details of the visit and what he'd said.

Pete paused only briefly before he said, "Don't worry about it."

Clearly Pete didn't understand the ramifications of what he'd done. "Yes, but—"

"What you told Mrs. Millstone was something I've wanted to say to her but lacked the courage. That old woman, God love her, needed to hear a few home truths, and you're just the one to say it to her. You're a better man than me."

"You're not upset?" Maybe Pete wouldn't be, but Hank knew Gracie wouldn't be nearly as forgiving.

"No, forget what happened and move on. Everything else going okay?"

"Other than Hortense escaping in the middle of the night, all is well."

"Grace Ann?"

Despite his worries, Hank grinned. "Is being Grace Ann. How about you? Anything exciting happening at The Last Call?"

"Yes, well, that's what I wanted to talk to you about. I hired a waitress."

Hank chuckled. "The customers a little too much for you to handle alone?"

"I needed help, that's for sure. It's Millie, the waitress from Mom's Place. She's a good worker and she needs this job. You'll keep her on after this week, right?"

"If she's all you say, then sure, no problem."

"That's a relief. Thanks, Hank."

"Thanks for understanding that I may have ruined your chance for a new church roof."

"Once I'm back, I'll do what I can to smooth Mrs. Millstone's ruffled feathers."

Hank was convinced it would be impossible to make reparations with the old biddy after the things he'd said. But if anyone was capable, it was Pete.

They spoke a few minutes longer. Hank had to swallow a laugh when Pete mentioned his altercation with the bikers from Hell's Outlaws. It seemed after only one day they had both learned valuable lessons about each other's role in life.

His amusement quickly faded as he approached the church office, knowing he would need to face Gracie.

He pasted on a smile, which quickly faded when she looked at him through narrowed, barely concealed angry eyes.

"What have you done?" she cried, and stood with her hands braced against her hips.

"Mrs. Millstone called?"

"Yes, and she said we could forget about any contribution toward getting a new roof for the church. She said she no longer wants anything to do with Peter or the church. How could you, Hank? You've ruined everything."

Watching Gracie blinking back tears nearly undid him. Still, he couldn't regret giving that old woman the tongue-lashing she deserved.

"I'm sorry," he said, and he genuinely was. "I should've kept my mouth shut, but I couldn't, seeing how mean and stingy she is toward her own family."

"We'll never get that roof for the church now."

Gracie was more upset than Hank had ever seen her. Hank hesitated. "Doesn't the church belong to God?" he asked.

"Technically . . . yes, but . . ."

"It seems to me," he said, "if God is who you say He is, then it makes sense to me that He knows that roof needs to be replaced and He'll see to it."

Gracie's mouth sagged open as if to argue.

"Either you trust Him or you don't. When I told Pete what happened, he told me not to worry, God provides. Think you could use a bit of that trust yourself." Having had his say, he left Gracie to think about finding the same trust in God that her brother had.

Grace Ann watched Hank leave and bit down on her lower lip. She'd been furious with him after Mrs. Millstone called the church office. The woman was outraged over the things Hank had said to her. Not only had she made it clear she had no interest in contributing to a new roof, but she also asked that her name be withdrawn from the church membership. This was bad. Really bad for the budget. She needed to connect with Leonard Fitzhugh, who headed up the finance committee. Worry settled between her shoulders like a sharp blade. The church would never meet their financial obligations without Mrs. Millstone's contributions.

And yet . . . what Hank said was true. This was God's church. It was His job to see the roof replaced. But how? She closed her eyes. No one else in Bridgeport had the means to help more than they already were. Faith. Trust. All at once, Grace Ann felt lacking in both.

CHAPTER NINE

Pete replaced the telephone receiver after speaking to Hank and was of two minds regarding their short conversation. His first thought was instant relief that his friend hadn't been upset that he'd hired Millie. If she worked as hard as she had the night before and proved herself this week, then he was sure Hank would want to keep her on. His relief on her behalf was huge. He didn't know what he would have done if Hank had said no.

The second part of the conversation weighed heavily on his heart. He'd flippantly claimed God would provide when it came to replacing the church roof. Now, after only a few minutes, major doubts had started to creep in. Mrs. Millstone was the main contributor to the church budget. A hundred times over the years he'd been tempted to say the very things Hank had and bit his tongue for fear of what it would mean to the workings of the church. What was done was done. He could try to apologize, eat humble pie, grovel with the hope she'd change her mind, but he doubted it would do much good. That woman had a streak of stubborn meanness a mile wide. No help for it now. Somehow, some way, he'd find the means to pay for that roof, God willing. Even while trying to have faith and think positively, the thought of losing Mrs. Millstone's funds filled him with dread.

He'd barely had time to sort through the ramifications when his phone rang. Even before he picked up, he had a strong feeling Grace Ann was on the other end of the line.

He was right. Even before she spoke, he could sense her outrage. "I know Hank already called you, but you will not believe what Hank has done now and—"

"Hank told me," he said, unwilling to listen to her tirade.

His interruption did little to cool her off. "Are you ready to admit this entire idea of yours and Hank's is an unmitigated disaster? One day, and look at the damage he's caused already. You've got to put an end to this madness."

"No."

His answer seemed to shock his sister, because the line suddenly went quiet. It surprised him because Grace Ann wasn't a woman who hesitated to speak her mind.

"Are you telling me you want Hank to stay on for the rest of the week? Right up until Christmas Eve?"

"I do. You and I both know Mrs. Millstone deserved every word Hank said. He's a braver man than I am. I admire the way he stood up to her."

"Even if it means we are out a new roof for the church?"

"Even then," he said, and he meant it.

Grace Ann hesitated and said, her voice almost a whisper, "I'll tell you what Hank said to me."

"I'm sure you will."

The sigh that followed said she didn't appreciate his sarcasm. "Hank basically said we should leave the problem with the roof up to God."

"Hank said that?" A slow smile came over Pete. His friend was right. The burden wasn't his to carry. "I have to say there are times when Hank shows more faith than me."

"And me," Grace Ann added.

Pete's eyes widened. It went against Grace Ann's nature to make such an admission. Maybe, just maybe, Hank was having a positive influence on his sister. He'd bit his tongue far too often when it came to her. It seemed Hank felt no such restraint. Once more, Pete silently applauded his friend.

"Anything else happening at the church that I should know about?" he asked, eager to change the subject. They spoke for a few minutes while Grace Ann updated him on the details around the live Nativity that would take place Christmas Eve. He didn't want to be rude and cut her off, but he was barely listening as she rattled on. He wanted to tell Millie, as soon as possible, that she had the job.

After what seemed like an hour, he was finally free. It was close to lunchtime, so Pete changed into a clean shirt and headed to Mom's Place so he could give Millie the good news. He felt almost giddy at the prospect of seeing her again.

Millie's circumstances had been on his mind all morning, and to be fair, a good portion of the night. She was strong and principled when it seemed as if the whole world was against her. How she'd managed to survive on her own for as long as she had was something of a miracle.

Pete deeply admired her, and if he was willing to admit it, he was strongly attracted to her, too. He'd noticed her long before and thought she was cute, and that was before he knew little more about her than her name. Seeing how pretty she was, he felt intimidated about asking her out. Still, he hadn't found the courage and was grateful for the opportunity to know her better.

This news could wait until she started work at The Last Call, but Pete couldn't. He drove the ten miles to Mom's Place, and the whole while his thoughts were on Millie. She lived from paycheck to paycheck. Christmas was just another day to her. On her tight budget, she wouldn't be able to afford a Christmas tree, let alone gifts. That seemed wrong. She deserved so much more.

Before he could change his mind, he stopped off at the local grocery store that sold miniature potted Christmas trees and picked out one decorated with tiny red glass bulbs. He'd give it to her when he drove her home that evening. He wanted her to know he liked her and felt at a complete loss when it came to expressing his feelings. After all her negative experience with men, he was unsure how best to convey his intentions and reassure her he was sincere.

As Pete approached the diner, he saw the six Harley motorcycles parked outside, and his heart sank. He wasn't sure he'd live through another run-in with these bikers. He parked and mulled over his next course of action. He focused his gaze on the painted Christmas tree that decorated the diner's window as his mind whirled with how to mend fences. It came to Pete that his scooting around the fact that he was a man of God had caused nothing but problems. He decided he needed to be honest and let the cards fall where they may.

The bell above the door jingled as he walked into the restaurant. The evergreen wreath swayed as he closed the door. Without hesitating, he walked over to the table where the six burly men sat. He pulled out a chair from an empty table and joined them without waiting for an invitation.

The conversation stopped, and all six men turned to stare in his direction.

"Good afternoon," he said, making sure he sounded friendly and comfortable, although he was anything but.

No one responded in kind.

Pete wasn't off to a good start. "I hope you'll excuse me for interrupting your conversation."

Silence again, although Snake half rose from his chair. He hesitated when he saw Millie as she came out from the kitchen carrying four plates. Two in her hands and two balanced on her arms. She stopped abruptly when she saw Pete, and her eyes seemed to ask him what he was doing.

"If you know what's good for you, I suggest you leave," Snake said.

"I promise I will, but before I do, I'd like to apologize for last night," Pete admitted. "I wasn't completely honest with you."

The six exchanged quizzical looks. "Explain yourself!"

Millie squeezed in between him and the bikers as she distributed the four large plates with cheeseburgers and fries. She caught Pete's attention and gently shook her head in warning.

Pete returned her look with a soft smile, assuring her he knew what he was doing. "Last night you asked me several questions, and I tried to make the answers as vague as possible. I should have been more up-front with you."

"And why would you want to cover up who you are?" Gunner demanded.

Millie returned with two more plates and stood at Pete's side after she delivered them. "There's a table open by the window," she said, gripping his shoulder.

"He's not going anywhere," Switchblade snapped back at Millie. "He has something to tell us."

"I said I was a teacher who taught ancient Middle East history," Pete reminded them.

Switchblade, who sat at his right, narrowed his eyes and snarled, "Trying to show us up like you've got a bigger brain than us."

"Actually, I wasn't, although it might have come off like that. The truth is I teach the Bible."

The silence that followed was as thick as the hamburger meat on their plates.

"You some kind of priest?" Snake demanded.

"Not a priest, a pastor."

"A what?"

"I'm the pastor at Light and Life church in Bridgeport."

The bikers exchanged glances, as if unsure what to make of his confession.

"I didn't exactly lie," Pete said, "but I wasn't completely honest, either. I apologize."

"A pastor . . . You mean like in church?"

"Exactly."

The bikers broke out in smiles and seemed to find Pete's confession amusing. "Get outta here."

"This is a joke, right?"

"It's true," Pete assured them.

"Stop it."

"What are you doing bartending at The Last Call?" Switchblade asked.

Pete smiled and explained how he and Hank had traded places for the week.

This seemed to confuse them. "Why would you do that?"

Pete shared the circumstances that had led him to take over for Hank for the week.

It seemed to hit Snake all at once. "You mean to say Hank is teaching the Bible to the good citizens of Bridgeport?"

"Not exactly . . ." Pete wasn't allowed to finish.

"This I've got to see."

"He's filling in for me this week," Pete continued, "but I'll be back in time for the Christmas Eve and Sunday service, and also the live Nativity scene Saturday night."

One of the men raised his hand and pointed at his burger and then at Pete, ordering him one.

Looking mildly relieved, Millie got the message and returned to the kitchen.

"Hank dealing with a live Nativity. This is gonna be good." Snake burst out laughing and slapped his hand against the tabletop as if he'd never heard of anything so crazy.

"It's not so nuts when you think about it," Pete said. "Both Hank and I deal in spirits. He's serving alcohol and I'm serving up the Holy Spirit."

"Hey, good one."

"I'd never have put you up against the dartboard if I'd known you were like a man of God," Snake said, and looked genuinely sorry. "God isn't going to hold that against me, right?"

"Of course not," Pete said, grinning that this man with the Hell's Outlaws etched on the back of his jacket was worried God would retaliate against him.

"We're good, then?"

"We're more than good.

"And as for you coming to see Hank, you're more than welcome to stop by the church anytime you wish."

"You don't mean that, Pastor. Look at us. All those

church people would go into convulsions if the six of us crossed the threshold."

"Put 'em to the test," Pete said. "We might surprise you."

They all chuckled like this was a good joke, only Pete wasn't teasing.

Millie delivered his cheeseburger and paused long enough to give his shoulder a gentle squeeze. He felt her warmth all the way to the bottom of his feet. A simple touch that almost took his breath away.

Pete and the bikers continued the conversation as they ate lunch. They didn't curb their need to use foul language or to tell off-color jokes. Pete didn't mind, because it meant they had accepted him. These men had something in common with Jesus; he was a rebel, too. Pete said as much, and that got their attention. Clearly this wasn't something they'd ever considered. He did ask that they not enlighten the patrons of The Last Call to the fact that he served as a pastor. They promised to keep the information to themselves, and Pete trusted they would keep their word.

They lingered over coffee, and Pete felt completely at home with them, and they seemed to feel the same way. His eyes followed Millie as she went about the diner, delivering meals and taking orders.

"I hope you come back tonight," Pete said, issuing an

invitation to the bikers. "Millie's working the bar and she can pour your beers a whole lot faster than me."

All six men smiled and nodded.

They stood as one to leave and slapped Pete across the back hard enough to displace his lungs, although he fought not to show it. Gunner insisted on paying for Pete's lunch.

As soon as the roar of their bikes faded, Millie started to clear off their table. "What just happened here?" she asked, as if she wasn't sure what to make of him.

"I made peace with the Hell's Outlaws."

She shook her head, as if she couldn't believe what she'd seen with her own eyes. "Those men are dangerous, Pete."

"Could be, but they didn't seem that way with me. They've chosen a certain lifestyle, and for that matter, so have I. We're still just men, and frankly not all that different. Yes, they swear, and their jokes would make Al Capone blush; it's true they might be involved in activities that could send them to prison, but on the inside, they're still just like you and me."

"I wouldn't count on that."

Pete didn't doubt that Millie had reasons to be skeptical. Her life hadn't been a cushy bed of rose petals. She'd been cast out into the world when she was still a vulnerable teenager and had done what she needed to do to survive. Pete wouldn't fault her for thinking the way she did.

"I almost forgot the reason I stopped by," he said, as Millie set the dirty dishes in a rubber tub. "I talked to Hank this morning about you staying on at the tavern after this week."

She stopped and turned to look at him, her eyes wide with anticipation. "What did he say?" She appeared to be holding her breath.

"He said if you were everything I claimed, he'd be happy to keep you on."

"That's great. Oh Pete, that's the best news ever." She tossed her arms around his neck and hugged him.

Pete's arms automatically went around her waist as he soaked in her relief and happiness. It felt good to hold Millie. It was as if she'd always belonged in his embrace.

"I don't ever want to go back to Toy's and there just aren't that many businesses that offer nighttime employment."

She broke away from his hold, and Pete was hard pressed to release her. If it was up to him, he'd want to keep her against him forever. The thought made him dizzy, and he felt the sudden need to sit down. He gripped the back of the chair until the sensation passed. He didn't know what was happening to him. All he knew was Millie was responsible for these strange feelings.

"I . . . I'll wait for you in my car," he said, breaking away.

"Wait for me?"

"I'll drive you to The Last Call so you won't need to take a taxi." Pete had to believe a good part of what she earned each day went to pay for transportation.

"You will?"

He nodded, finding it hard to speak.

She went still for a moment. "You don't need to be so kind to me, Pete."

Her words soaked into his heart. "I rather think I do," he said, and left the diner, his heart pounding in his chest.

He had the car warmed by the time Millie left the restaurant. She opened the passenger door and spotted the tiny Christmas tree Pete had purchased in the seat.

"This is so cute," she said, lifting it so she could slide into the car.

"Actually"—he paused and cleared his throat—"I got it for you . . . I hope that isn't inappropriate, I mean, it is a little forward of me to assume, you know, that you would want this little tree. I thought, you might, you know, not have a Christmas tree of your own and—"

"Pete," she said, cutting him off.

He met her gaze.

"I love it. Thank you. I think this is the sweetest thing anyone has ever done for me." Tears welled in her eyes, and she sniffled and blinked furiously, as if to hold the emotion at bay.

"I didn't mean for you to cry, it's just that I saw this and hoped it was something you'd enjoy. The truth is, I've thought of you a lot, even before you came into The Last Call, but I didn't know—"

Turning in the seat, Millie pressed her finger against his lips. "Stop," she said softly.

"Stop talking? I do that when I'm nervous, my sister says—"

Millie pressed her finger a little stronger over his lips, silencing him. Holding his gaze for a moment, she leaned forward and gently kissed him.

Pete kept his eyes closed, savoring her kiss.

"Was I being inappropriate?" Millie asked.

He beamed her a smile. "If so, could you be inappropriate again?"

Millie laughed and nodded. "I'll see what I can do."

CHAPTER TEN

Present Day

Nana looked to Lance. "You can take your fingers out of your ears now."

"This kissing part is over?"

"For now."

"You mean there's more?" He groaned with the question, as if this was too much romance to endure.

"Nana, I like Millie best," Lily said, ignoring her brother. "And Peter seems to like her best, too."

Nana squeezed her granddaughter's shoulder. "Millie is a good person who's down on her luck. Getting that barmaid job made a tremendous difference to her entire future."

"Is that because Peter falls in love with her?"

"No, no, please," Lance insisted. "Nana, please!"

"I gave you fair warning, Lance, and I will again if it's necessary."

"So, they do kiss again?" Lily gleefully clapped her hands.

"They do," Nana said, "again that very night."

Lance groaned, sank down on the sofa, and placed his hands over his ears. "I don't want to hear it," he said, sounding annoyed.

Nana had trouble holding back a smile.

Undeterred by her brother's attitude, Lily tugged on Nana's sleeve. "I bet it happened when Peter drives Millie home from work that night."

Her granddaughter had a romantic heart. "You're right. Millie worked hard to prove herself because she badly needed that job."

"And she didn't want to go back to that awful place where she worked before, right?"

"Right. She was grateful to Peter for helping convince Hank to let her keep the job."

"She kissed him first, though?"

"Yup, and then he kissed her again and again and told her how much he liked her. That was the night he told her that he hoped at the end of the week, she would be willing to date him."

"Nana." Lance groaned in protest, removing his hands

from the side of his head. "This isn't the way the story is supposed to go."

"Why not?"

"It's getting mushy. I want to hear more about the bikers."

"I'll get back to them in a little bit. Okay?"

Heaving an exasperated sigh, he continued, "All right, but I don't want to hear about any more kissing."

"For now," Nana promised.

Lily was having none of it; she longed for more details. "So, what happened after Peter kissed Millie?"

"Well, Peter was so happy that the next morning he called his sister and told Grace Ann all about Millie and that he intended to date her."

Lily frowned. "I'm not sure I like Grace Ann. She's too . . . fussy."

"That she was," Nana agreed, "but you wait, she eventually comes around."

Lily looked skeptical, as if she wasn't sure Grace Ann could change. "What did she say when Peter told her he was going to date Millie?"

"She didn't think it was a good idea, did she?" Lance asked, fidgeting. "How much longer before the bikers come back?"

"Not long, I promise, and Lance, you're right about Grace Ann."

"Did she pretend to be happy for him?"

"Not in the least. Actually, she said very little, but Peter got her message. He didn't care though, he was smitten."

"What's smitten?" Lance asked, cocking his head to one side.

"I bet it means he likes Millie," Lily explained to her brother.

Lance scooted down and covered his ears again. "Wake me up when you get to the part where the bikers come back into the story."

"Oh, I think you'll like this next part best," Nana told him.

"Why? What happens?"

"You'll need to listen to find out."

"Let me guess," Lily said, sitting upright and full of enthusiasm.

"What do you think?"

"It's Grace Ann, right? She gets mad that her brother wants to date Millie."

"Could be. You'll both just need to wait to find out. Now let's get back to the story."

CHAPTER ELEVEN

"You wanted to see me?" Hank asked, coming out of Pete's small office, where he'd been reviewing the church's budget. Seeing the numbers and the balance sheet had been an eye-opening experience. From what he could assess, there was little wiggle room when it came to paying for anything outside of the listed expenses. Since he was the one responsible for the loss of funds for the new roof, he'd been hoping to find an area where the church could make up the difference. As best he could tell, there wasn't one. He did have a few ideas, though.

Gracie, prim and proper as always, said, "Leonard Fitzhugh has called an emergency meeting of the finance committee to meet here within the hour."

"For?"

"Isn't it obvious?" Gracie said through pinched lips. "Without Mrs. Millstone's help, the committee needs to discuss how best to move forward in regards to the badly leaking roof."

"And how is it Leonard knows about Mrs. Millstone's decision?" He suspected Gracie had made sure to gleefully report Hank's run-in with the cantankerous widow.

"Well . . . I felt it was only right that he and the other committee members know what's happened."

Hank suspected her motives were less than stellar. Gracie was looking to put him on the hot seat. Make him pay for his misdeeds by having to own up to the good men of the community for what he'd done.

"Perhaps it would be best to have Pete join us," Hank suggested.

"He can't."

"And why's that?" If he were to guess, it was because Gracie hadn't mentioned the meeting to her brother.

"He's busy."

That sour look Gracie sometimes got was back. "Is there something you want to say?" he prodded, because clearly there was.

"What do you know about this woman Peter hired?" she demanded with pinched lips.

"Not much. Pete told me she'd been working a second job at Toy's and—"

Gracie gasped and her hand flew to her heart. "The strip club?" For a minute, it looked like Gracie was about to hyperventilate.

"Yes. Do you have a problem with that?"

"My brother . . . and a stripper?" Gracie buried her face in her hands. "This is too much."

"Gracie Armstrong, aren't you being just a tad judgmental?" Hank asked, leaning against her desk. "Millie works as a waitress for the lunch hour at Mom's Place. She's a good employee and was down on her luck. Your brother gave her an opportunity. I don't understand why you're so upset."

Gracie lowered her hands from her face. Hank noticed she'd gone pale. "Peter . . . Peter told me he's going to date her."

Hank grinned, happy to hear his friend had found the courage to approach Millie. From conversations over the years, he knew none of the women Pete had dated in the past had spurred an interest. Millie did; he'd noticed it that very week when they'd met for lunch. Hank was pleased and thought, wrongly, it seemed, that Gracie would be, too.

"Kindly wipe that smug look off your face," Gracie snapped. "This is a disaster in the making. What do you think the good people of the church will say if they were to learn my brother was dating a stripper?"

He let the fact that Millie wasn't a stripper slide. "In my humble opinion, why should it matter?"

"Who cares about your opinion?" she shot back, as if this was exactly what she'd expected him to say.

"Right." He didn't attend the church and knew only a few people in Bridgeport. But he could see her point.

"This is horrible," Gracie said, as if she was close to tears. "I can't let Peter do this. Something has to be done. Sooner or later word is going to get out. People are going to talk. What can Peter say after rejecting several eligible women in town? Godly women who attend this very church?"

"If I were Pete, I know what I'd say," Hank offered.

"Really?" The lone word dripped with sarcasm. "I can well imagine." She rolled her eyes at him.

"Yes, really. I'd say what Jesus did and ask who'd be willing to throw the first stone."

Gracie's eyes widened, and then her mouth dropped open as if she had something to say and then changed her mind. She glared at him as if his words had cut her to the bone.

"Not everyone was raised with the love and support you got from your family, Gracie. All I know about Millie is what Pete mentioned, but it's clear she hasn't had an easy time in life. Your brother has a good head on his shoulders and generosity of spirit, which it saddens me to say you unfortunately seem to lack. Pete's an excellent judge of character. If he's attracted to Millie, the former waitress or whatever it was she did while employed at Toy's, then I think you should trust your brother's judgment. I'm happy for him, and you should be, too."

He expected Gracie to speak her mind. She hadn't held back to this point. To his surprise, she lowered her gaze and kept her thoughts to herself.

Before Hank could continue, she turned back to her typewriter and whispered, "Leonard and the rest of the committee will be here soon."

"Thanks. Let me know when they arrive."

Without looking at him, Gracie nodded. Hank hoped he'd given her something to think about, although he wasn't sure he'd gotten through to her. Her lack of a response told him nothing.

Sure enough, about twenty minutes later, Gracie informed him the committee had arrived and had gathered in the small conference room in the back of the building.

Three men looked up when Hank entered the room with the church budget he'd studied earlier. He extended his hand to the first man. "Hank Colfax," he said, introducing himself.

"Leonard Fitzhugh." The two exchanged handshakes.

"Hello, Ken," he said next, addressing his old high school classmate.

Ken nodded.

"Jerry White," the third man said.

Hank pulled out a chair and joined them at the table. "From what Gracie said, you know Mrs. Millstone has decided she no longer wishes to fund the new roof for the church."

Three gloom-filled faces stared back at Hank.

"So we heard," Leonard muttered.

"I take full responsibility for her change of heart." He picked up the budget he'd recently reviewed. "If you don't mind, I have a few questions for you."

"Fire away," Ken said, and gestured toward Hank.

"What's your break-even point?"

"Our what?" Ken and Jerry looked back at him blankly while Leonard seemed to be studying the tabletop.

"How many supporting church members do you need to meet this budget?"

The three men stared back at him with blank looks. Jerry shrugged, and so did Ken.

Leonard spoke for the three: "I can't rightly say."

"Do you have a profit-and-loss statement?"

Again, he got blank looks in return.

"How is it this church stays afloat?" Hank wondered out loud.

"Faith," Ken told him.

"Faith is all good and well, but you're going to need to

work this out. I apologize for speaking my mind to Mrs. Millstone and ruining your chances of getting that roof. My guess is Mrs. Millstone has held a lot of sway with the church. Giving her that much power isn't good for anyone."

Leonard sighed and nodded. "I've been thinking the same thing for a long time but never had the nerve to say it out loud. You're right. That disagreeable old woman has run Pastor Pete ragged demanding almost constant attention. He's had to kowtow to her for far too long. Never met anyone so miserly and mean in my life."

"She's miserable and wants to make everyone else as miserable as she is," Hank offered. "I should have held my tongue, and I apologize for the predicament I've put the church in with my loss of self-control."

"No need to apologize," Jerry said.

"Jerry's right. You only said what most of us were thinking anyway," Leonard assured him. "If anything, I think Pastor Pete will be grateful to be out from under her thumb."

The men of the finance committee relaxed and grinned.

"I would have loved to have been a fly on the wall," Leonard said, and chuckled softly.

"It's been my experience that God will make a way where there isn't one," Jerry added. "Somehow, some way, we'll get that new roof. We can worry and fret about it or we can put our faith to work, stand back, and let God do the rest. However, if you have any ideas, we'd be open to listening to them."

"As a matter of fact, I do have one idea. Have you thought about holding a bingo night? The church has the space for it in the meeting room. The kitchen is an asset; you could sell popcorn and hot chocolate. Sell sandwiches and whatever else you like. Not only would it be a moneymaker, but you'd offer a social activity when there are so few, especially in the winter."

The men exchanged looks. "What a great idea."

"And just think about all the people it would bring into the church," Leonard said, nodding as he spoke.

"Right." Jerry was in full agreement.

"I wish I'd thought of that," Ken added. "It would do me good to see Mrs. Millstone's reaction when she sees the church's new roof."

"And seeing that we're all here," Ken said, "why don't we lend Hank a hand in distributing the charity baskets?"

"Good idea," Jerry said, standing up from the table.

The mood had shifted from when Hank had first entered the room. The relief was palpable, with almost a sense of excitement floating in the air. These men of faith and their willingness to listen to his idea inspired Hank.

As the four left the conference room, Gracie looked up

and frowned in confusion when she saw their smiling faces. She blinked several times, as if she didn't know what to think.

"I'll be out of the office for the foreseeable future," Hank said as he passed her desk.

"See you later," Jerry said, as he walked past her and out the office door. Ken, Hank, and Leonard followed.

All Gracie seemed capable of doing was staring at them, apparently speechless. That had to be a first. It was enough to make Hank struggle against showing his amusement.

The four divided up the charity baskets into teams of two. Jerry and Leonard went in one vehicle and Hank was grateful to spend time with Ken. He had a few questions for the other man regarding his relationship with Gracie. While she hadn't said anything about the other man, claiming they had been nothing more than friends while in high school, he'd seen her reaction. It seemed to him there was more to the story.

Hank offered to use his truck, and after dividing up the baskets and the addresses, the four of them drove toward their assigned residents.

As they pulled away from the curb, Hank looked over at Ken. "Heard you were in Nam."

"I was. That's where I met my wife. Fell in love with her the moment we met."

"That's great, Ken."

"Meeting Lieu was worth every minute in that hell hole."

Hank could see his schoolmate had found his soulmate. "Did your family have any problem accepting her?" Hank had heard some families had a hard time adjusting to foreign wives when their sons returned from the war.

"Mom and Dad didn't, but, well, you might remember I dated Grace Ann for a time in our senior year."

Hank had graduated by that point, but he thought he remembered there'd been something going on between Gracie and Ken, regardless of what she said. Now that was confirmed.

"Was it serious?"

Ken hesitated before responding. "More so on her end than mine. She wrote me every day after I got drafted, and I appreciated her letters. I was away from home for the first time and hearing from her helped ease the homesickness. She filled me in on what was happening in Bridgeport and the local news. It was like getting a piece of home with every letter."

Hank nodded, encouraging Ken to continue. "Then I got shipped to Nam and met Lieu. Her name means willow tree. I fear I handled the situation with Grace Ann poorly. She continued to write and signed every letter *with love*. I didn't want to mislead her, so I stopped writing. Oh, I'd answer her every now and again, always coming up with an excuse as to why I took so long to respond."

"When did you tell her about Lieu?"

"I didn't," he said, his voice heavy with regret. "Like I said, I messed up big-time."

Things were starting to add up in Hank's mind. Gracie must have felt betrayed. Next to no letters from Ken. No doubt she worried and fretted when she didn't hear from him. "When did Gracie find out about Lieu?"

Ken hung his head. "When I returned with my wife. I know she was shocked. I regret that I didn't have the courage to tell her beforehand."

"What happened then?"

Ken looked out the passenger window. "Nothing. She never said a word, and I didn't, either."

Silence hung between them as Hank absorbed the information.

"Thanks, Ken. I appreciate your honesty," he said after a few uncomfortable moments.

"The thing is, Grace Ann changed after that," Ken said, as if he carried the weight of what had happened. "Pastor Pete knows it, and so do I. She was always . . . you know, proper, I guess you'd say. For the last few years, she's been closed off from almost everyone. The only thing she really seems to care about is playing the piano for the church and the Ladies Missionary Society, which she leads. I don't know that she has any real friends any longer."

Hank had noticed the same things. The church was Gracie's life. She'd buried her head in the sand when it came to relationships, and life in general.

No wonder she was worried about her brother dating Millie. Pete was more than her brother; he was her only friend. If the church objected to Pete dating Millie, he might choose to leave as their pastor. If he did, Gracie's entire world would fall apart. Where would she go? What would she do? How would she support herself?

Admittedly, Gracie was a complicated woman. Even knowing what he did, Hank was convinced that behind the wall she'd constructed around her heart, she had a lot of love to give.

Tapping his fingers against the steering wheel, Hank wondered what he'd need to do to breach that wall. In the same breath, he decided he wasn't going to back down until he dug deep enough to find his way to the real Gracie Armstrong. The Gracie he remembered and had always enjoyed.

CHAPTER TWELVE

Pete had barely slept. After kissing Millie, he hadn't been able to stop thinking about her and how much he savored their exchanges. He never expected she would battle tears over the gift of the small Christmas tree he'd impulsively bought.

Later, after the tavern closed and he'd driven her home, they'd kissed again with several deep, breath-stealing exchanges that left his head and his heart spinning. Pete had returned to his car, and it felt as if he was walking on air. He'd kissed women before. The experience was not new to him, only this time it felt that way. Millie's touch had burned through him like fire, awakening in him such joy; it was all he could do not to skip to his vehicle like a kindergartner on the first day of school. When he did finally fall into a light slumber, his dreams were full of Millie. He couldn't wait to see her again. Couldn't wait to find out if she was as impacted by their exchange as he'd been. Even thinking about her sent his heart racing, and she was rarely away from his thoughts.

As he had the previous day, Hank called Pete first thing that morning. "How's it going?" his friend asked.

"Good. Better than good."

This was surprising. "Really?"

"I mean it, Hank. We did a booming business last night. Hell's Outlaws were back, and since I'd cleared the air with them, they were great. They aren't so intimidating as I first thought. Other than their language and a few bad habits, they aren't that different than you and me."

"It sounds like you've made friends with the bikers?"

"We have an understanding."

"Guess that means they aren't using you for dart practice?"

"Nope. And Millie's a great help. She's an asset; everything went much smoother with her at my side."

"Glad to hear it."

"Listen, I'm glad you called, because I have an idea I want to pass by you." This was something that had been brewing in Pete's mind all morning, and he needed Hank's okay before he mentioned it to anyone.

"Sure. What's up?"

"I was talking to Millie and Snake, and it came to me that the bikers, and the regulars like Walt and Rowdy, don't really have the same opportunities you and I do to celebrate Christmas traditions. To them, it's simply another day of the week."

"You want to invite them to church?" Hank sounded skeptical. "Don't take this wrong. It would be fine if you did, but I don't see Snake and the others hanging around the live Nativity scene."

"I don't, either. I thought I'd bring Christmas to them."

Hank went quiet, and Pete thought he could hear his friend scratching his head. "How do you intend to do that?"

Pete would need help, and already his mind was working on how best to make that happen. "I'd like to throw a Christmas party at The Last Call. A few games, some holiday drinks, a little food, and music. It wouldn't be Christmas without the carols. I notice you've got a piano tucked off in the corner."

"That old thing hasn't been played in years."

"Grace Ann can tune it." That might take a bit of persuasion on his part—actually, a lot of persuasion. Once his sister understood why it needed to be in playing condition, she would have a hard time saying no. That was his hope, anyway. One could never be certain when it came to Grace Ann.

"From what I've seen of Gracie, it would take a miracle to have her tune that relic. She is one stubborn woman."

Hank wasn't telling him anything Pete didn't already know. "What do you say about the party?"

"I think you should go for it. I'll stop in myself, and if I can convince her, I'll bring Gracie with me."

That would be the day! "Walt and Rowdy will be happy to see you. They've been quite vocal, asking when you're going to return."

"Are those two old coots giving you trouble?"

"Nothing I can't handle," Pete said, grinning as he spoke. The two regulars had gained a soft spot in Pete's heart with their complaints and their adversarial friendship with him and each other.

"And listen, speaking of Gracie . . ." Hank started to say, and paused, as if he wasn't sure how best to continue.

They hadn't been speaking of Gracie, which basically told him his sister was the real reason behind Hank's call.

"What has she done now?" Pete understood his sister could be a real piece of work. From the beginning, she'd been against the idea of him and Hank trading places. He'd hoped his friend would be a good influence on Grace Ann. She needed her tidy world shaken up a bit, and Hank was just the man to see to it.

"Two things," Hank continued. "First off, she let the

finance committee know that I'd blown it with Mrs. Millstone. After they learned what I'd done, Leonard called an emergency meeting to review the budget. I studied it myself, hoping to find a way to cut expenses so the church could afford the new roof. I came up with a couple ideas to help. I only hope it's enough." Hank went on to explain his thoughts and the finance committee's reaction. Pete mulled the idea of a bingo night, and a smile came over him. Grace Ann might disapprove of gambling in the church hall. Nevertheless, if it kept the heat on and the church from going under, his sister might have a change of heart.

Seeing how tight finances were, it must have come as a surprise to his business-minded friend. "There's never been much wiggle room in the budget."

"You're telling me!" Hank said. "I don't know how you are able to keep everything going as it is. So do you think a bingo night would work?"

"I do."

"You could sell a few snack items, too."

"That's another great idea."

The budget had always been month-to-month, but Pete had learned to trust God for the church's needs. There'd been times when he wasn't sure they could pay the light bill, and yet God has always come through. Not once had Pete been let down. Yes, there'd been a few times when he'd had to take less for himself in order to keep the heat on. It hadn't been a big deal. Pete was willing to do whatever was necessary for the church to remain open. He wondered why he hadn't thought of a way to supplement the income before, and was grateful for his friend's ideas.

"God will make a way where there is no way. If He wants to use bingo, I'm all for it."

"Great," Hank said, as if relieved.

"Was there something else?" Pete asked. He remembered Hank had mentioned two things that were on his mind.

Hank's sigh was deep and troubled. "You can blame me for this, so I apologize in advance."

This didn't sound good.

"I mentioned Millie to your sister, and the fact that she worked at Toy's, and Gracie about had a conniption."

Pete's heart sank. His sister would need to find out about Millie sooner or later. However, he would have preferred to be the one to tell her. It was too late for that now; the deed was done. It didn't take much to know what her reaction was.

"Don't worry about it," Pete said, with more confidence than he was feeling.

"You know Gracie better than me, but if I were you, I'd gather my gear for battle," Hank continued. "For reasons I'm only beginning to understand, she feels threatened by this."

Pete did know his sister, and while he loved her, no way was he willing to let her dictate his life.

"From Gracie's reaction," Hank continued, "it wouldn't surprise me if she showed up at the tavern sometime today."

Pete planted his hand on his forehead. Having his sister give Millie a hard time wasn't something he would allow. Hank was right; he needed to be prepared in advance. "Thanks for the warning."

"And while we're discussing Gracie, you should know I had a long talk with Ken. From what he said, she seemed to have read more into their relationship than warranted. When he returned from Nam with a wife in tow, it seems Gracie didn't have a clue he was with someone else."

"I know." Peter had prayed endlessly for his sister and her reaction to Ken's marriage. She refused to speak about it, instead bottling everything up inside. While she was polite when forced to be around the couple, he noticed how she avoided them as much as possible. With Ken on the finance committee, that made it difficult. Almost always, Grace Ann found an excuse to be away from the office when their meetings were held.

"I like Gracie." Hank's words were heartfelt.

"You do?" His friend's tone suggested Hank had romantic feelings for Pete's sister and was more than just friendly. It took a moment to get over the surprise of a possible romance between Grace Ann and his best friend. After the shock, his first thought was that Hank was exactly the kind of man his sister needed in her life.

"She's a challenge, that's for sure," Hank said. "I doubt she'd ever consider dating me, but I won't let that stop me."

"Don't give up."

Hank chuckled. "You know me better than that."

"I do," Pete agreed, wondering what it would take to open Grace Ann's eyes to the possibilities of a relationship with Hank. "And I'll keep an eye out for a visit from Grace Ann today. I appreciate the warning that she might make a showing."

They were both silent for a bit, mulling over their conversation. "Everything good at the church?" Pete asked. Until this week, his entire life had revolved around his role as pastor and the activities that went on there.

"Swimming along." Hank sounded confident, as if his obligations had been a breeze, which Pete knew had to be an exaggeration. "The charity baskets got delivered. I showed up for choir practice last evening and checked in with the folks who volunteered to be at the live Nativity on Christmas Eve. Word around town is that swarms of people are coming from as far away as Colville."

"Looks like you're filling my boots without a hitch."

Hank emitted a scoffing laugh. "I might have ruffled a few feathers along the way through no fault of my own, just ignorance."

"No word from Mrs. Millstone, I take it?"

"Nope. I'm afraid that ship has sailed." Hank was apologetic. "No thanks to me."

"You know, it's a funny thing," Pete said. "Not having to worry about offending Mrs. Millstone is something of a relief. She made me grovel for every penny she donated. You might think you were out of line, Hank, but actually, you did the church a favor."

"That helps ease the guilt, although I doubt Gracie sees it that way."

"That's unfortunate . . . sad, really." Pete wished he knew how best to reach his sister. Every time he tried to talk to her about her future, the discussion went south. Hank wasn't the only one who'd noticed the changes in Grace Ann. Pete suspected her reluctance to open up to him was because they were too close. He spent more time with his sister than anyone. He prayed that in time she'd be willing to loosen up a bit, and, knowing Hank, he felt his friend was just the man to do it.

Hank had given Pete quite a bit to think about. He needed to be prepared to face his sister. It was necessary she understand he wasn't going to change his mind when it came to his feelings toward Millie. She might object, but Pete was hopeful that once she met Millie, Grace Ann would have a change of heart.

They spoke a bit longer, as Pete clarified what he intended for this Christmas party. Hank was fully on board and thought it was a great idea. His enthusiasm spurred Pete's imagination, and before he knew it, Hank had agreed to the extra expenses for all his friend planned.

The rest of his morning was spent getting the tavern ready to open in the afternoon. Pete made a couple signs announcing there would be a Christmas party on Friday and that all were welcome. A few calls to friends in Bridgeport followed. Those he spoke with were excited at his suggestions and promised to do what they could to make this special party something the tavern patrons would long remember.

When he picked up Millie after her shift at Mom's Place, she was all smiles. Matter-of-fact, so was he. He casually mentioned the party, wanting to gauge her reaction.

"A Christmas party?" She clapped her hands, letting her enthusiasm show. "Oh Pete, that's such a nice thing to do. If you want, I could bring the tree you gave me and help with the decorations."

"A tree," he repeated. They would definitely need a tree, but not a miniature one. He'd get the biggest tree he could find.

With a mental jolt, he realized he might have taken on a bigger project than he realized. Of course, they needed decorations. If he was going to put on a Christmas party, they would need something to lend spirit to the celebration. Already his mind was whirling; Millie inspired more ideas in him.

"We'll get a real tree," he said. "A big one so high it will touch the ceiling." He didn't want her to give up the one piece of Christmas he'd gifted her.

Sure enough, not ten minutes after The Last Call opened for business, Grace Ann arrived in a whirlwind, marching in the front door like a general calling the troops into battle.

She ignored Millie and made her way over to Pete. "We need to talk," she said, and after pointedly looking toward Millie, added, "privately."

Walt and Rowdy exchanged glances and Walt said, "Looks like someone got a stick up their—"

Before he could finish, Grace Ann whirled around to face the two men. "I beg your pardon! What did you just say?"

"I didn't say anything," Walt muttered, and practically buried his face in his beer.

Rowdy seemed to find something of interest that

needed to be scraped away with his fingernail on the top of the bar.

"You must be Grace Ann," Millie said, greeting his sister. "I'm Millie." It took all the restraint Pete could muster not to leap in front of Millie to shield her. Instead, he stood by her side and placed his arm protectively around her middle.

His sister seemed to have lost her voice, which under any circumstances was highly unusual. Grace Ann had rarely showed restraint when something was on her mind.

"I'm happy you stopped by," Peter said, waylaying her. "The old piano here needs tuning. I don't know anyone more qualified to see to it than you." His sister had been gifted with perfect pitch and had been the one to tune the church's piano for years now.

"You want me to do *what*?" she asked, clearly taken aback by his request.

"Pete is hosting a Christmas party here on Friday," Millie explained, her eyes bright with excitement. "It would be wonderful if you'd come and play for us. He's told me how musical you are. It's such a pleasure to meet you."

Millie seemed determined not to let his sister intimidate her, although he noticed that she trembled slightly. It seemed from the time she'd left home Millie had learned to stand up for herself.

"Peter told you about me?" Confusion flickered in Grace Ann's eyes as she looked from one to the other. "I can only imagine what he said."

"He mentioned how efficient you are and how much of a help you are to him at his"—she paused and glanced toward Walt and Rowdy—"other job. He said he couldn't accomplish half of what he does if it wasn't for you."

The frown Grace Ann wore relaxed slightly as she looked in her brother's direction. "Peter said that?"

"He's most appreciative."

Peter was afraid of what Grace Ann would say next. She'd arrived for the sole purpose of reminding him that his association with Millie would likely cause him to be let go as the Light and Life pastor. He didn't believe that for a minute. He knew his congregation, and he trusted his friends. But he was willing to let the cards fall where they may.

Before Grace Ann had the chance to say anything more, the door opened with a cold blast of winter air. Three women who wore heavy makeup, faux fur coats, and fishnet stockings came into the tavern.

"Millie," one the girls cried out, rushing over to hug her.

Pete stepped aside as the three circled Millie. They all seemed to be talking at once. From what he could make out, they were friends of Millie's who worked at the strip club.

"I was sick when I heard what happened."

"The only thing that rat, Clint, said was that you weren't coming back."

Millie hugged each woman and then introduced them to Pete and Grace Ann. "These are my friends from Toy's."

Pete noticed how pale Grace Ann had gotten and shot her a look that warned her against saying a single word.

"This is Stacy, who goes by Kitten onstage." Millie indicated the tallest of the three.

"Hi," Stacy said, and raised her hand.

"And Bonnie, whose stage name is Angel."

Grace Ann muffled a cough and Pete poked her side, afraid she was about to make some comment over Bonnie's stage name.

"And Lucy," Millie continued, "who's also known as Candy." Millie looked toward Pete. "Lucy is Snake's girlfriend."

"Snake?" Grace Ann asked, staring at Millie's friend. "What kind of name is that?"

"He's the president of Hell's Outlaws," Lucy proudly explained.

For just a moment, Pete thought his sister would faint. The look she gave him said volumes.

"These are my closest friends," Millie said. "I'm so sorry I had to leave without explaining. I couldn't take serving there a minute longer, and you know what? It's worked out for the best. I got a job here at The Last Call so now I don't have to deal with those . . . men."

"Snake is the one who told us where you went," Lucy said. "We've all been so worried."

As if suddenly remembering her manners, Millie gestured toward Grace Ann and Pete. "This is Pete and his sister, Grace Ann. She is going to help us with a Christmas party here at The Last Call," she said.

"Hello," Grace Ann returned, sounding as if she'd swallowed something that had gotten stuck in her throat.

"Oh," Millie added excitedly to her friends. "You have to come. Pete is getting a huge tree, and there's going to be cake and cookies. It's going to be a real party, and Grace Ann is going to tune the piano and play carols and we're all going to gather around it and sing."

Their eyes brightened.

"What about work?" Bonnie asked, as the enthusiasm drained from their faces one by one.

"Call in sick," Millie said.

"We don't work, we don't get paid."

"It's Christmas," Millie countered. "You must come. When was the last time you attended a Christmas party?"

Millie's friends snickered. "Like never," Stacy murmured.

"Then you'll do it?"

The three exchanged glances before smiling. "We'll be here."

"Wonderful." Too excited to contain herself, Millie hugged each of her friends in turn. Then she looked to Grace Ann and wrapped her arms around her. "Thank you so much," she said.

Grace Ann managed a weak smile before she muttered something Pete couldn't hear. He watched as his sister walked out of the tavern looking something akin to a Halloween zombie.

He noticed Millie wore a puzzled look. "Everything okay?" he asked.

"I think so," she said. "Your sister whispered something I didn't quite understand."

Pete bristled. "What did she say?"

Millie shrugged. "It didn't really make any sense; it was something about throwing stones?"

CHAPTER THIRTEEN

When Gracie disappeared from the church office Thursday afternoon, Hank knew where she'd gone. Not for a moment did he doubt she'd taken off for Kettle Springs to confront Pete about his romantic interest in Millie. Pete could hold his own against his sister, of that Hank had no doubt. He'd heard the determination in his friend's voice when it came to his relationship with Millie. If anyone knew Pete, it was Hank. No way would his friend back down, even if it cost him professionally.

Hank had located the sheet Gracie had created that dutifully listed his assignments for the week. He visited the sick, checked the church furnace, which, as best he could tell, was on its last legs. This was likely its last winter before it gave up the ghost. Another worry Pete would face in the coming months. Hank had had no idea of the heavy load his friend carried.

Checking the list twice like he was the man in the red suit, Hank finished everything that was required of him by midafternoon. As best he could determine, the rest of the day was free. Good thing, because he had plans. Thursdays were poker days, and he'd convinced his buddies to drive into Bridgeport for their weekly game. They were feeling generous about coming the extra twenty miles since he was on a losing streak.

When he returned to the office, Gracie was sitting at her desk. She looked up when he entered and tossed him an accusing look.

"This is all your fault, you know."

He raised his arms as if she'd pointed a gun at him. "What did I do now?"

Her look said he knew exactly what she meant. "It's all because of you that my brother is about to ruin his reputation."

"Oh, and how's that?" he egged her on, knowing how much she enjoyed berating him.

"Peter is associating with strippers, and even invited them to that Christmas party he intends to have. It's ridiculous."

He raised his index finger to shut her down before she got carried away, which for Gracie didn't take much.

"Millie is a woman down on her luck, looking to make a better life for herself."

"In a strip club?" Gracie's eyebrows threatened to meet her hairline.

"Clearly you've never been in a desperate situation."

Gracie opened and closed her mouth. It went without saying that by comparison, Gracie had been brought up in a loving family with all the comforts that afforded her.

The tightness around her mouth eased and she looked down at her typewriter keys. "I'm worried what consequences this association will have once the congregation learns that Peter is dating . . . this woman."

For the life of him, Hank couldn't hold back his amusement.

"Do you think this is funny?"

Despite his effort to appear serious, his mouth quivered with a smile he found impossible to suppress. "I suppose in a way I do. Gracie, come on, think about this. You should be happy for your brother."

"Happy?" Her eyes rounded as if she'd never heard anything more outrageous.

"Did you meet Millie?" Hank asked. While he hadn't paid much attention to her as the waitress at Mom's Place, he trusted Pete's judgment.

Gracie stiffened her shoulders until she resembled a raw recruit standing at attention before a drill sergeant.

"I met her and . . . her friends. The strippers who've been invited to his Christmas party."

Understanding was beginning to dawn on him.

Gracie arched one brow. "I suppose you're well acquainted with Kitten, Angel, and Candy, which I was informed are their stage names."

It appeared Gracie had gotten the full introduction. Hank could only imagine her response to these women. "And?"

"And what?"

"Did they have horns coming out of their heads?"

"Don't be absurd," she snapped.

"So what's the problem?"

She stared at him as if he was purposely being thickheaded. "The problem . . . these women—"

He didn't let her finish. "Millie's friends are strippers, and you're better than they are, is that it? Holier? A saint, while they're sinners? You attend church, and they entertain men, which makes them too dirty for you to associate with?"

Likely because she didn't have an answer, Gracie ignored the question. "Millie wants me to tune that old piano for this party my brother is intending to throw. Heaven help us. I can't imagine what Peter is thinking. I can't. I simply can't be party to this. My brother has lost his mind, I tell you. As far as I'm concerned, you're to blame."

Hank shrugged off her comment, because frankly, he couldn't disagree more. Nor was he going to listen to her tirade any longer. It was time he set her straight.

"It's been a while since I last opened my Bible," he admitted.

"I have no doubt." She was so full of self-righteousness she was practically choking on it.

"Perhaps so," he said, amiably enough, "but I do seem to remember that Jesus was friends with prostitutes and tax collectors."

She glared at him, and he noticed her ears had turned a deep reddish color. "I hate it when you do that."

"You mean remind you of what the Good Book says?"

"You know exactly what I mean." She flared, and whirled around in her chair, giving him the view of the back of her head.

"You should accept that with or without your help, this party is going to happen."

"Peter doesn't need me."

"He needs you to tune the piano, and he wanted to include you. Because of your brother, Millie, Kitten, Angel, and Candy are probably going to attend the best Christmas party of their lives. You can join in or stay home and revel in your holiness. While you're there, I suggest you read your Bible; it might enlighten you to a few home truths."

Gracie had nothing more to say, it seemed, which was

fine by Hank. He didn't know how much more of her holier-than-thou attitude he could take. He'd said his piece and doubted it'd had much impact on Gracie.

With a sigh, he added, his voice low, his anger gone, "I'll be around if you need me."

"I can assure you I won't."

"Well, then, have a good afternoon." He'd tried to reach her and was beginning to think he'd wasted his breath.

"Do you think I could have a good afternoon after this?" she snapped.

Shaking his head, Hank left her alone to stew. Those concrete walls of hers seemed to grow thicker by the day. He'd made little to no progress in his effort to break through to her heart.

An hour later, Hank let Snake, Gunner, and Rowdy into the church building via the back door. No need to rile Gracie more than he already had. It was just as well that Gracie was upset, because she hadn't come to investigate his visitors. He led them into the conference room and closed the door.

"This the church?" Rowdy said, looking around.

"We're inside the building, but this is the conference room. It leads to the inside of the church."

"Never set foot inside one in my life," Gunner said, checking out the room like he'd walked into a dark cave and was bound to get lost in the interior.

"Me, neither," Snake added. "You sure God doesn't mind us playing poker in here?"

"I doubt it. If Jesus was around, He'd probably join us."

"That would be cheating, because He'd know all our cards."

Hank laughed. "You're right about that."

The four gathered around the table for their weekly game. Hank had brought the chips with him and the cards, too. He shuffled and dealt out the first hand. Thirty minutes later they were well into the game when the door to the conference room opened.

Like an avenging angel, Gracie stood in the doorway and her mouth sagged open at the sight of Snake with his leather vest and his heavily tattooed arms. Rowdy set his cards down on the table.

"What's going on here?" she asked, looking to Hank for an explanation.

"It's a poker game," he told her.

"In the church?"

"The conference room," he corrected.

With a pause she said, "I'm going to need you and your friends to leave."

Hank shook his head. "Not happening."

"The Ladies Missionary Society meeting is scheduled for this afternoon. The ladies are due to arrive in fifteen minutes."

"We can't quit now," Gunner insisted. "I'm holding a full house."

Far be it from Hank to disrupt the Ladies Missionary Society meeting. "We'll finish the hand and move the game to the parsonage." It would be a tight fit around the kitchen table, but they'd make it work.

Gracie nodded, and her eyes avoided his. Something was different in her. He didn't know what it was. He intended to find out, though.

As his friends vacated the church and headed to the parsonage, Hank stopped off at Gracie's desk.

"Thank you," she said.

"No problem. You and your lady friends have a good meeting." He hesitated before adding, "It's wonderful that the church cares for those hurting and in need around the world. But Gracie, there's a mission field right here in Bridgeport and in Kettle Springs. You seemed to think you're above Kitten and the rest. Better. Holier. Yet I can't help wondering, given the same circumstances in life they've had, what you would do."

Gracie turned away, and Hank sighed inwardly. It didn't seem he would ever reach her.

Hank and his friends finished the poker game at the parsonage. His losing streak continued; the cards, however, weren't the problem. His mind was elsewhere, on Gracie. He'd expected her to have a fit when she realized he had a card game going in the church, even if it was the conference room. Yet when she'd come upon them, she'd seemed almost subdued. That wasn't like her.

After his buddies left smiling with their winnings in hand, Hank returned to the church. Gracie sat at her desk and didn't look up when he came into the office.

"How did the Ladies Missionary Society meeting go?" he asked, watching her closely.

"Fine." She didn't sound like herself and kept her head lowered, avoiding eye contact.

"Gracie?"

She sniffled, reached for a tissue, and wiped it under her nose. "What?"

"Are you . . . crying?"

She swiveled her chair away from him. "Don't be ridiculous."

"Look at me," he instructed, his voice gentle, concerned.

"No." The one word was more sob than sound.

"Gracie?" He tried again. "Look at me."

"Please leave," she pleaded, and buried her face in her hands, her shoulders trembling as she wept.

Seeing her like this broke Hank's heart. Coming around the desk, he knelt in front of her and reached for her hands, tenderly tugging them away from her face. Tears rained down her cheeks, and her nose was red. It seemed she'd been crying for some time.

"Gracie, what's happened?" he asked in a whisper. Finding her sobbing was the last thing he'd expected.

"You," she cried, and reached for another tissue before she loudly blew her nose. "Please leave . . . I don't want to talk to you."

"I don't think I can go."

"Why not? Do you want to torture me even more?"

He continued to hold her hands in his, his fingers enveloping her much smaller ones. "How am I torturing you?"

Shaking her head, she refused to answer him. The sobs started anew.

"Talk to me. Please," he added.

"You're right . . . so right."

"About what?"

She shook her head and then appeared to change her mind. "I've become like one of the Pharisees. I'm critical and judgmental. I'm a hypocrite," she confessed between soft wails.

He released her hands and cupped her face. "Gracie, you're beautiful."

"Stop it."

"You should know by now I don't hedge around the truth." Seeing how blunt he'd been with her, she had to realize he said what he meant.

She sniffled again. "I look a sight. I've never been one of those women who cry pretty. My nose runs, and my face gets all blotchy, so if you think I'm pretty, then you are badly in need of glasses."

"I've never seen you look more lovely." It was the plain truth. His heart felt like it'd grown to twice its size. He found he couldn't look away, drinking in the sight of her, red nose and all.

Before he could talk himself out of it, he leaned forward and pressed his lips to hers. Her mouth fit his perfectly, and he sighed when after only a second or two of hesitation, she hugged his neck.

Hank had waited a long time for this moment, and he had no intention of rushing it. He stood, taking her with him, bringing her body flush against his. The kisses continued, one following another. Hank couldn't get enough of the taste of her. The way he felt in that moment, he could kiss her all the way into eternity.

When they broke off the kiss, Gracie buried her face in his chest. Her sobs had subsided, and she ran her tongue over her lip as she looked up at him with tear-filled eyes. "What you said earlier . . ."

"I'm sorry if I hurt you."

"You hit the mark," she admitted, and sniffled. She wiped the moisture from her cheeks with one hand and held on to his shoulder with the other. "You're right about me, so right. I've turned into another . . . Mrs. Millstone."

Hank grinned and shook his head. "I wouldn't go quite that far."

"You're wrong. I . . ."

"You wrapped your religion around you like an iron shield," he supplied. Worried as she was about everything, she forgot the most important aspect of what it meant to be a Christian: living a life of faith.

"I have closed myself off from everyone," she whispered. "It's because . . . because I was in love once, and I thought he felt the same way about me. Only he didn't. When I learned he didn't care the same way I did, it broke my heart. I thought . . . assumed if I was a better person . . ."

"Shh." He pressed his fingertip against her lips. "I know."

"You know?" Her gaze shot to his.

He nodded.

"You can't . . . I never said anything, not even to Peter."

"I talked to Ken."

Her eyes nearly bulged from her head. She broke their embrace and retreated a step. "You had no right."

"Perhaps, but there was a problem, you see?"

"What kind of problem?" she asked, her gaze full of skepticism.

"I was falling in love with you, and I couldn't seem to get past the barrier you'd erected. I needed to find a way to your heart, so you'd give me a chance."

All the doubt faded from her expression. "You love me? How is that possible? I've been wrong about so many things. And the way I've treated you . . ."

"You're Gracie, and I have to say I had no difficulty falling for you. Honestly, I was halfway there when we were in high school. Only you were Pete's little sister, and I wasn't sure how he'd feel about it."

"You liked me all those years ago and never said a word?"

"Pete was pretty buff back in those days, and after three years in braces, I valued my teeth."

Gracie broke into a laugh, and because he couldn't resist, he kissed her again. He smiled to himself because he was convinced he could hear the wall around Gracie's heart cracking wide open.

CHAPTER FOURTEEN

Present Day

Her young grandson dropped his hands from protecting his ears and heaved a loud sigh. "I don't know why anyone would ever want to kiss a girl."

Nana didn't bother to hide her smile. "You won't always feel that way, trust me."

"Nope, never gonna do it." He made a disgusted face and shook his head as if he'd bitten into something rotten. "Yuck. I'm disappointed in Hank. I thought he was smarter than to fall for Gracie."

"I think Hank is wonderful," Lily said, with a deep, romantic sigh. "If I was Gracie, I'd let him kiss me."

"I liked him well enough," Lance said, "until he got caught up in all that mushy stuff."

"I like this story, Nana," Lily said, ignoring her brother.

"What about you, Lance?" Nana asked. "What do you think about the story thus far, discounting the parts where there are kisses?"

"I liked it when Hank was caught playing poker in the church. I want to hear more about Snake and Gunner."

"You will, I promise," Nana assured him.

"I didn't like Grace until now," Lily added. "She was so . . . stodgy."

"Stodgy?" Nana repeated. "That's a big word for you."

"I heard it on television and asked Mom what it meant."

"Good for you."

Lance crossed his arms and rolled his eyes.

"Lance doesn't know any big words," Lily said, and stuck her tongue out at her brother.

"Do so," Lance argued.

"No arguing," Nana chastised them both, "otherwise I won't finish the story."

"Oh, Nana. Did Gracie tune the piano for the party?"

"She did."

"I thought she would, because Hank kissed her."

"It was more than Hank's kiss. She had an epiphany."

"A what?"

"Her eyes were opened to what she'd become, and that

made all the difference to Gracie and her attitude toward Hank and her brother's new friends."

"I still don't understand why she was so . . ."

"Stodgy," Lance supplied, as if to prove he knew big words, too.

"Well," Nana explained, "Gracie had been hurt, and sometimes when someone is disappointed in life, they protect themselves so no one else can ever hurt them again."

"Is that what Gracie did?"

"Yes, and because she did, she missed out on many of the good things that were available for her."

"Like falling in love?" Lily asked.

"She got Hank," Lance reminded his sister.

"Yes, in the end she did get Hank," Nana agreed, "but before he came along, Gracie avoided anything that would endanger her heart. She closed herself off from friendships, made up excuses to stay home, and did everything she could to prove how worthy she was of love. Deep down, I believe she wanted Ken to regret choosing someone else to love other than her."

"Can we get back to the story, Nana," Lance said, clearly wanting to avoid any more talk about love.

"Sure thing."

"I want to hear about the Christmas party," Lily said, scooting closer to her Nana.

"Did the bikers come?" Lance asked.

"They sure did."

"Did they play darts?"

Nana smiled. "They didn't, because they were having too much fun doing other things."

"I like Christmas parties," Lily said.

Lance made a scoffing sound. "Everyone likes parties, what's not to like? There're desserts and presents."

"Were there presents at the party?" Lily turned her head to look at her Nana.

Nana nodded. "There were, and you'll never guess who brought those."

"Tell me!"

"I will. That's all part of what happened next."

"All the kissing is over, right?" Lance wanted to know.

"There might be a little bit at the end, but I promise to give you fair warning."

Lance raised his hands, ready once again to cover his ears.

CHAPTER FIFTEEN

"Never been to a Christmas party before," Walt told Pete, leaning against the bar as he nursed a frothy mug of cold beer.

Pete suspected few of Hank's customers celebrated Christmas, at least in the traditional sense. He figured they were aware of the holiday. It was hard to miss, with all the store displays and the lights that decorated Main Street. But he was convinced that few of his new friends sat down to a turkey dinner with all the trimmings or shared the holiday with family or friends.

"I heard you were gonna put up a tree."

"Planning on it," Pete told him, as he filled the orders Millie delivered. Over the past few days, he'd become proficient in pouring beer from the tap. He wasn't as fast as Hank, and probably never would be. Bartending wasn't exactly his calling in life; nevertheless, he'd learned a great deal in the three days he'd taken over for his friend. He had to assume that his counterpart had come away with a few lessons of his own. He'd been surprised by how smoothly Hank had filled in for him. Oh, there'd been a few bumps along the way. His sister had been more than happy to fill him in on all Hank's misdeeds, although Pete didn't view them that way.

For his own part, he realized how reluctant some people from church were to discuss their troubles with him. They put on a good front, when all the while, they dealt with their problems on their own. Not so at The Last Call. A good example was the trucker who stopped in earlier that afternoon. Looking as if he hadn't a friend in the world, the trucker had sat down at the bar, ordered a brew, and then poured his heart out. The poor guy's marriage was in trouble.

He didn't know Pete. The two had never set eyes on each other. Pete listened, nodded now and again, and then asked a few questions about the length of time he was away from home and how his wife dealt with the children while he was gone. The questions were subtle and appeared to set the man to thinking. After thirty minutes or so, the trucker was back on the road. His step was lighter, and he thanked Pete for listening. Had he known Pete pastored a church in Bridgeport, it was highly unlikely he would have been nearly as open.

The only people aware that Pete was a man of God were the men from Hell's Outlaws, and they'd given him their word that they wouldn't mention it to anyone. And, of course, Millie knew.

The trucker wasn't the only one who eagerly shared their secrets and woes. Since he'd been at The Last Call, Pete had heard Rowdy's life story and some of Walt's, too. Both men had served in World War II and were full of tales from battles where they'd engaged the enemy. Their marriages hadn't lasted, and they'd lost track of their children while drifting from one city to another, and job to job, finding work wherever they could.

"It isn't too late to connect with your daughter," Pete had told Walt. The old geezer immediately rejected the idea, adamantly shaking his head.

"She hates me."

"So you've been in touch with her."

"No, haven't seen her since she was six."

"So how do you know she hates you?"

Walt hesitated. "If she doesn't, then she should. I've been absent nearly her entire life. She probably doesn't even remember me."

"You sure about that?"

"Sure enough. Her mother remarried as soon as the

ink was dry on the divorce papers. Susan had a new father; she didn't need me."

"It won't hurt to reach out."

Walt hung his head. "I never was much of a father."

"It's Christmas," Pete said, "and hearing from you might be the perfect gift for Susan."

Walt grew quiet and seemed to mull over Pete's words. After a few minutes, he sniffled and wiped his nose with the sleeve of his wool shirt.

Rowdy slid onto the stool next to Walt. "You got a cold?"

Walt ignored the question and sipped his beer. "None of your business."

Millie returned to the bar with an order, her face bright with a smile. "Everyone is talking about the party, Pete," she said, her beautiful blue eyes glowing with excitement. "Kitten stopped by on her way to Toy's and several of the girls have decided to take the night off."

Pete was pleased to hear it, although it added extra pressure for him to make this party something special.

"Clint is losing his mind with so many of the girls taking off. He treats them all like they're dispensable. It's time he realized he wouldn't have a club without us girls."

Pete was busy filling her order and worked to hide the stress he felt after suggesting this party. "It serves Clint right," he said, as he placed the filled pitcher on her tray.

"This party means the world to the girls, Pete. Thank

you for doing this. I've never heard my friends this excited about anything."

Pete had come up with the idea on the spur of the moment, without giving it much thought. He'd wanted to do something special for the people he had come to care about since taking over for Hank. Mostly he'd wanted to give Millie the Christmas she deserved.

"We're going to have a full house tomorrow night for sure," Millie said, as she lifted the tray from the bar and disappeared into the crowd.

Pete swallowed tightly. His idea had been to put up a tree, sing a few carols, and make a toast of Christmas cheer. One beer on the house. Only it had quickly turned into something far and above what he'd imagined. He was going to need help. Lots of help.

From the way Grace Ann had reacted to his idea, he doubted she'd be willing to lend a hand. Pete had come to rely on his sister for a great many things over the years. Now he stood alone, and he was worried.

As usual after closing for the night, Pete drove Millie home. She chatted the entire time, full of excitement over the party and Christmas. Once at her rental, she turned to look at him and smiled. She placed her hands on both sides of his face and kissed him.

"Thank you, Pete, for everything." She said this with tears of gratitude clouding her eyes.

Pete watched her enter the house and remained parked

out front until her lights went on. A crushing weight landed on his chest. He was drowning and unsure what to do. Before the panic set in, he did the one thing he knew would help. Pete bowed his head and prayed, asking God to help him throw a birthday party for baby Jesus that Millie and all their friends would never forget.

After a sleepless night of tossing and turning, caught between praying and worrying, he woke and immediately called Hank. His friend had barely answered when Pete said, "I'm in over my head."

"What?" Hank asked, as if he didn't have a clue what Pete was talking about.

"The Christmas party . . . I . . . I—"

"No worries," Hank interrupted. "We're coming."

How could Pete not worry? He'd made a simple suggestion and it had gotten out of hand. He was in dire straits. Heaven help him; he'd never thrown a real party in his life. The expectations weighed him down like concrete boots. He needed help and he needed it big-time. All at once, what Hank said permeated his brain.

"We?" he repeated. "You and who else?"

"Gracie," Hank said, as if he should've understood.

"You mean she's willing to tune the piano?" He'd count his blessings if she'd do that one thing. Anything more was above his expectations.

"Yup, and more."

Pete was shocked. "But I thought . . ."

"Gracie and I had a come-to-Jesus talk."

Pete was speechless. Hank talking to Grace Ann about faith? His imagination ran wild. He couldn't fathom what Hank had said to his sister that convinced her to help with this party.

"Did you hear me?" Hank asked.

"Yes, but what happened? I know Grace Ann and—"

"It will take too long to explain. Listen, don't panic. Gracie is working her organizational magic. We'll arrive around one with plenty of help."

"Help? You mean there are more than you and my sister who are willing to lend a hand?"

"Yup. She reached out to the Ladies Missionary Society. From what I understand, they are all bringing baked goods. The church ladies decided it's all well and good to support foreign missions, which they have done for years. I helped them look at the mission field that's right here in Bridgeport and Kettle Springs."

Once again Pete was speechless. "I hardly know what to say."

"Don't say anything. Gracie and I will head out as soon as we have what we need."

Relief washed over Pete, and when he hung up the phone, he turned his eyes toward heaven and whispered, "Thank you."

CHAPTER SIXTEEN

Sure enough, a few hours later, to Pete's relief, Gracie arrived. When she walked in the door it took a moment for Pete to recognize his own sister. Nothing physically had changed about her that he could detect. It was in the way she glowed and smiled. That prim, sour look she'd worn for the last several years was gone. He wanted to ask her what had happened, and would later, when they had a private moment.

First thing, she dusted off that old upright piano, sat down, demanded silence, and tuned it back into playing order. When she'd finished, she ran her fingers over the ivory keys as she played one of their favorite Christmas carols, "It Came Upon the Midnight Clear." When she finished, she glanced over her shoulder and smiled at Hank, who was quick to return a grin of his own.

Hmmm. That was interesting. His friend walked over to Grace Ann's side and placed a hand on her shoulder before bending down to kiss her.

Pete nearly dropped the string of lights he'd been about to place around the window. Hank straightened and seemed to feel Pete's gaze. He joined Pete at the front of the tavern.

"Do you have a problem with me dating your sister?"

Pete didn't need to think twice. "Truth be known, I think it's great. You're exactly the right person for Grace Ann." He'd thought that more than once through the years. And been tempted to mention it to Hank, but had resisted. Grace Ann had closed herself off from relationships to the point she bristled every time he mentioned it, and so he'd given up.

Hank looked more than pleased. "I'd like to think that's true. I guess time will tell."

Hank had always had a more easygoing nature. He didn't take life nearly as serious as Grace Ann did. However, seeing the smile on his sister's face convinced him something good had shaken her awake.

Hank glanced at his watch. "I'm heading out to pick up the tree with a couple guys from the church."

"You managed to round up more volunteers?"

Hank's smile widened. "You haven't seen anything yet."

Pete had to wonder what Hank had up his sleeve.

An hour later, Hank had returned, dragging one of the tallest Christmas trees Pete had ever seen. He needed help simply getting it through the door. Ken was with him and Jerry White, too. It took all three men to set it in place, and only after they'd moved the pool table to the other side of the tavern to make room.

When he first saw the tree, Pete was convinced it would never fit. But they were able to wrestle it inside and needed to cut off only the very top in order to make room for the star.

Grace Ann supervised the three men, and after the tree was in place, Pete noticed his sister pull Ken aside. Curious, he kept an eye on her as the two spoke privately. He'd always wondered about his sister and the local deputy. They'd dated in high school, and she'd mentioned writing to him while Ken was in Nam. Although Grace Ann had never said anything after he returned with a wife, Pete had the feeling Ken had deeply wounded his sister's heart. He'd tried to ask her about the relationship once and she'd nearly bitten his head off. Not wanting to be a pest about it, he'd dropped the subject.

Grace Ann and Ken spoke for several minutes and then hugged. Pete glanced toward Hank and noticed that his friend had taken note of the conversation himself. Hank didn't show any concern, though. In fact, he looked pleased.

Shortly before the scheduled opening, Grace Ann's friends from the Missionary Society filed into the tavern, with their arms loaded down with a variety of items. Soon the entire countertop of the bar was piled high with a wide variety of cookies and Christmas candies.

Pete hated to leave, but Millie would need a ride from Mom's Place. He smiled the entire ten-mile drive, believing God had worked a miracle not only in his sister's life but in his, too.

As soon as he pulled into the parking lot, Millie raced out of the restaurant. "I'm so sorry," she rushed to tell him as she slid into the front seat of his car. "I tried to get off early and couldn't. I know you need my help and I feel like I let you down."

"It's fine," he told her. He hated to see her frazzled and concerned.

"It isn't. You can't get everything ready on your own. Mom's was slammed. I couldn't believe how busy we were."

"Millie, I have help."

Her eyes doubled in size. "You do?"

"Grace Ann and—"

"You mean your sister . . ." She paused, as if she didn't believe him. "After yesterday, I didn't think she wanted anything to do with me or . . . or any of my friends."

"That was yesterday," Pete said, grinning as he spoke.

Miracles happen, and he'd seen not one but two, all in a short amount of time.

"What changed her mind?"

"I wasn't sure until a few minutes before I left to collect you. I believe my little sister is in love."

"She loves you and wants to do this for you," Millie guessed.

"Yes and no. Hank is the one who convinced her to help. I believe there's a bit of mutual admiration going on between them."

"Wow, that's great."

When he pulled into the tavern's parking lot there were several vehicles taking up space. The party had yet to start and already people had gathered, waiting for Pete to open the front door.

Knowing what was happening inside with the decorations and everything else, Pete could hardly wait for Millie to see it all for herself. The place had been transformed into Christmas Central.

Millie walked through the front door and froze as if in shock. Before her was the huge Christmas tree where the pool table and dartboard had once been set up. It was covered with lights, ornaments, and tinsel. Spread below the tree were dozens of wrapped packages. The windows were outlined with flashing, colorful lights, and wreaths hanging in the middle of each one. An evergreen bough stretched from one end of the bar to the other.

"Come in," Grace Ann said, walking over to Millie and taking both her hands. "We could use your help."

"Okay," Millie said. Her voice was more whisper than sound. "What do you need me to do?"

Pete stopped her long enough to help her remove her coat. He couldn't stop smiling. This was above and beyond anything he could have imagined or hoped for this party.

The church ladies were amazing. All too soon, Millie and Grace Ann were busy decorating the tables. There were candy canes and candles, red and green balloons, and treats. The home-baked cookies and candies had been divided among the tabletops until there was barely room for anything else.

The Last Call opened its doors at seven that evening. A long line had formed outside. Hank stood with Pete as everyone piled in from the cold. Pete didn't even mind the blast of frigid air as they held the door open.

The first one in line was Walt, with Rowdy following close behind him. Both men paused to look around and then grinned at each other. It didn't take them more than two seconds to find a table and start munching down on the cookies. Pete recognized the small round ones his mother called snowballs, dusted with powdered sugar. The powder stuck to Rowdy's beard like frost.

The men from Hell's Outlaws followed, and they, too, paused in the doorway to look around. They nodded approvingly and moved inside.

Most everyone who showed up was someone Pete recognized. If he didn't, Hank did. They greeted each person individually.

When Kitten entered the tavern, she covered her mouth with both hands. "Lucy, look, a Christmas tree with lights and everything."

Grace Ann sat at the piano playing Christmas carols. A few of the church ladies stood around the old upright, enthusiastically singing. It wasn't long before others joined them. Some knew the words; others didn't.

"Time for the first game." Hank shouted to be heard above the cacophony.

"Games?"

"I need the ladies from Toy's," Pete said, standing in front of the bar.

Not knowing what to expect, the ladies glanced from one to another. After a brief hesitation, six of the women stepped forward.

Next, Hank asked for Grace Ann to join the women. The strippers were dressed in short skirts, black knee-high boots, and faux-fur jackets. Grace Ann wore her Sunday best, a floor-length high-waist dress with a Santa hat. The contrast couldn't have been more striking.

Two of the women from the church, women Pete had

dated at one time or another, removed six of the wrapped gifts from beneath the Christmas tree.

"Presents?" Kitten breathed out and clapped her hands excitedly. "We get presents?" Chatter immediately broke out.

Hank held up his hand to garner their attention. "Yes, but you have to work for them."

Lucy eyed Hank through narrowed eyes. "If you're going to ask us to strip, then save your breath."

"I wouldn't dream of it."

"Good thing." The six strippers gathered around the table with the gifts.

"Like I said," Hank continued, "these gifts are yours, but they might not be as easy to open as you think."

Grace Ann stepped forward with six pairs of oven mitts, which she handed to each of the strippers.

"The first one to open their gift gets an additional present from under the Christmas tree."

All six stepped closer to the table, mitts on their hands. From the eager look about each one, they didn't need an extra incentive.

Those at the party gathered around the women and then Hank said, "On your mark, get set, go!"

The women did their best to tear aside the wrapping paper to the cheering and encouragement from the crowd. It seemed useless, until Kitten, not about to lose out, bent over and used her teeth to tear away the wrapping paper. The other five women quickly caught on and did the same. Because she had the edge, Kitten managed to get the present opened first. With her hands free now, she lifted the lid to the box, and then slowly raised her eyes, seeking out Grace Ann.

"It's bath salts and scented soap." Kitten brought the bar to her nose and breathed in the scent of rose perfume. "I've never . . ." For only a moment, tears glistened in Kitten's eyes.

The other women were finally able to open their packages. Each gift was different. Special and thoughtful. The women hugged them to their chests and laughed, showing them off like they'd found buried treasure.

Pete had wondered at the games Grace Ann had chosen, thinking they might be a bit unsophisticated for this crowd. To his surprise, they were a huge hit. Pin the Hat on Santa reminded him of his first night at the tavern, when Snake, Gunner, and the rest of their crew had used him for dart practice. He smiled now as he watched the hard-core bikers blindfolded. They took the game seriously, and after being spun around, aimed for the head of the large picture of Santa. Hoots of laughter followed as Santa was covered nearly everywhere but his head, and in some rather intimate areas, as if that was the point of the game.

After the gifts had been distributed so there was one for each person, they gathered around the piano and sang more Christmas carols. Several, singing loudly and off-key, were creative in supplying their own unorthodox lyrics.

Pete saw his sister blush a few times. To her credit, Grace Ann didn't comment. Hank hovered at her side and often had his hand on her shoulder, as if he felt the need to be close. Pete watched as the two exchanged looks every now and again. Warmth exuded from his friend and his sister. It was the same way he looked at Millie.

She stood close to Pete. He reached for her hand as the singing continued, and they exchanged smiles. He wanted to kiss her, to tell her how special she was to him, only that would need to wait until a more appropriate time.

A free round of beer was served, and then the huge sheet cake was brought out, lit with two dozen candles. Cake and beer. Who would have thought of enjoying the two together? Strange as it might seem, for this night, this party, beer and chocolate cake complemented each other.

Once the cake was eaten and the beer enjoyed, Hank got everyone's attention. He stood on a chair to look out over the partiers. He put two fingers to his lips and produced a piercing whistle.

"I have an announcement to make," he called out, as he garnered attention.

The room quieted as friends looked expectantly at him.

"This week you met my friend Pete," he said.

Several people raised their empty mugs and gave a shout of approval.

"Pete Armstrong has been my best friend for nearly my entire life. Come here, Pete," Hank said, and gestured for him to stand on a chair beside him.

Pete did as Hank requested and looked quizzically in his friend's direction.

"Two things I want to mention about Pete. First off, I've had a thing for his sister since our high school days."

The crowd cheered, and Pete watched as Grace Ann's face turned three shades of red. Even though she was embarrassed, he didn't miss her smile. She blew Hank a kiss and Hank beamed a smile in her direction.

"As you already know," Hank continued, "I've been away from The Last Call for the week. Pete filled in for me."

"Pete's okay. Not as good as you when it comes to pouring beer. When are you coming back?" The comment and question came from Rowdy.

"December twenty-sixth."

"Why so long?" Walt demanded. "You're usually open Christmas Eve."

"Not this year." Again, Hank's attention focused on Grace Ann. "This year I've got plans. I'm going to church."

"Church?" Walt snapped, as if he couldn't get the word out of his mouth fast enough.

"Pete's church. That's the other bit of news I wanted to share. Pete Armstrong is the pastor at Light and Life church in Bridgeport."

A stunned silence fell over the group before a wave of murmurs broke out. Snake stepped forward and announced, "Me and my club knew all about it," as if having insider information was his due. "Pete and Hank decided to trade places this week. Been an experience, hasn't it?"

Pete laughed. "It sure has been."

"You're a man of God?" Walt looked like he was about to spit.

"Yes. Just a man, though, like you. No better, no worse."

Walt continued to stare at him through narrowed eyes, which Pete ignored. "Hank's coming to the Christmas Eve service at the church tomorrow night, and I want to personally invite each of you."

Grumbling followed, and he noticed several conferencing with their neighbors and then shaking their heads. The response didn't look positive.

The party wound down and gradually people started to leave. The strippers were the first to go. Pete had the impression they were headed back to Toy's to make the most of what was left of the evening. They hugged Millie, and to his amazement, Grace Ann, too, before they headed out into the cold.

Hank, Pete, Millie, and Grace Ann were the last ones to head out. Exhausted and exhilarated from the party, Hank decided to clean up the tavern the next day.

"Thank you for all your help," Millie told Pete and Grace Ann. "The night was magical thanks to you, and Hank, and all your friends. This was a party none of us will ever forget."

It was one that would linger long in Pete's mind and in his heart, too.

CHAPTER SEVENTEEN

Hank stood in the middle of his tavern and grinned despite the mess and clutter left behind from the Christmas party. The success from the night before lingered in his mind, producing a warm feeling. Even now he found it a little short of shocking how his friends and customers had taken to Pete's idea. Despite their often-crusty exterior, the tattoos, and their defiant attitude, the bikers and the rest were all children at heart, looking to celebrate the season.

Never in a million years could he imagine the Hell's Outlaws, standing around the piano, singing Christmas carols. True, their words didn't exactly match the traditional ones. Remembering Gracie blushing at some of the more inventive phrases caused Hank to chuckle out loud. Bless Gracie. Hank knew she'd had to bite her tongue more than once at some of the colorful language. He was likely the only one who noticed how red the rims of her ears were.

The ladies from Toy's were another surprise. He was overwhelmed that the lure of a party had brought them to The Last Call and that they'd given up a night's pay. Despite the heavy makeup and revealing attire, they were all little girls at heart, looking to be included in the holiday spirit.

The best surprise, and one he would long treasure, was his Gracie. His heart warmed just thinking about her. When he'd stood before his friends and announced he'd always had a thing for her, it was no joke. He didn't know what had transpired between her and Ken earlier that day when she'd pulled the deputy aside to talk. Hank would have liked to have been able to listen in on the conversation.

Whatever was said appeared to have cleared the air. Hank was reluctant to admit that when they'd hugged, his first reaction had been jealousy. Amazing how quick that green-eyed monster reared its ugly head. Unable to stop himself, he'd taken a step forward, needing to stake his claim, then realized it wasn't anything he needed to be concerned about. One step and then he stopped. Ken was a happily married man. The hug Gracie gave him was her way of taking back her heart. Good thing, because Hank was more than ready to lay claim to it himself. When she looked his way, he smiled, letting her know he understood and was grateful the two had cleared the air.

The tavern wasn't going to clean itself with him standing around musing about the surprising events from the night before. The good feelings would last, though. Heading into the back room, he grabbed the broom and dustpan. He was about to tackle the mess when there was a loud knock against the front door.

Before opening it, Hank looked outside the window to find Pete's car parked there. Turning the lock, he let his best friend inside.

"What are you doing here?" Hank asked; this was unexpected. The switch was over. It was Christmas Eve, and Pete had a sermon to prepare.

"You didn't think I'd leave you to clean up alone, did you?" Pete said, taking in the chaos left behind from the party.

"Don't you have duties in Bridgeport?"

"I do. Grace Ann is filling in for me with the dress rehearsal for the Sunday-school kids. They're practicing for the Christmas play. I figured you could use a helping hand here, seeing this party was my idea."

Not tarrying to chat, Pete went about clearing off all the tabletops and depositing the mugs and other glassware in the dishwasher.

"What about your sermon?" Hank didn't want Pete to feel obligated to help him when he had a message to prepare.

"Short and sweet, just the way the congregation likes my sermons. I wrote it a couple weeks ago. The main part of the service will be the Sunday-school kids' reenactment of the Christmas story."

"I appreciate the help," Hank told him, "but please, if you need to be elsewhere, go. I can clean this up in no time."

"I'm good. I just have to collect Millie after her shift at Mom's, so no sweat." Pete carted another tray of empty beer mugs toward the bar.

Hank continued working, lifting the chairs and turning them upright to place on the cleared tables. Wrapping paper littered the floor, along with smashed cookies and heaven knew what else.

"That was some party, wasn't it?" Pete commented, looking pleased with himself.

"The best," Hank agreed.

"I couldn't have pulled it off without Grace Ann," Pete admitted, as he continued with his cleanup efforts. "My sister is a marvel, the way she rounded up the ladies from church and put them to work."

Hank was in full agreement. "How those church ladies managed everything within a few hours is nothing short of amazing."

"I don't think they're finished yet, either."

With one of the chairs in his hands, Hank paused and looked over at his friend. "What do you mean?"

"I mean Gracie's friends intend to keep in contact with the women at Toy's. They want to love on them, show them how precious they are."

Hank frowned. "I don't think Kitten and the rest are much interested in being evangelized."

"Don't think that's the intention," Pete explained. "The church ladies want to gain their trust so the girls at Toy's will feel comfortable to talk and share their lives with them. Gracie told me next week they plan on giving the girls pedicures. It's a woman thing. One-on-one."

"I imagine Gracie is spearheading this group."

Pete laughed. "How well you know my sister."

Hank hid a smile. He did know Gracie.

"I can't imagine what you said or did, Hank. The change in Grace Ann is night and day. She's got a completely different attitude toward just about everything. What happened?"

"Well, other than my come-to-Jesus talk, not much. Like you said, Gracie was caught up in being perfect in every way."

"Legalist," Pete supplied. "It was as if she needed to prove she was better than everyone else in order to feel loved."

Hank agreed. "Unfortunately, in the process, she lost sight of what it means to be a Christian. And happy."

Pete's look was thoughtful. "Whatever you said had a powerful impact on her."

He could have talked until he was out of breath; it wouldn't have made a bit of difference if Gracie hadn't been ready to hear it.

"All Gracie really needed," Hank said, "was someone to point out the truth." He knew some of the things he'd said had been difficult for her to hear. And it was even harder to own what she'd become. He was afraid that at the rate she was headed, Gracie would eventually turn into another Mrs. Millstone.

Remembering the bitter old woman caused him to cringe. Although Pete had absolved him of guilt over the loss of funds for the church roof, Hank still felt bad. With his own finances stretched, there was no way he could afford to help. Then he remembered the very thing he'd told Gracie. If God didn't want His house to have a leaking roof, then He would take care of it. Easy to point out and equally difficult to let go and let God. Trusting didn't come easy.

Working side by side, it didn't take more than ninety minutes to get The Last Call clean and ready for business after Christmas Day.

Pete looked at the time. "I'd best leave now. I'm bringing Millie to Kettle Springs to spend the next couple days with Grace Ann and me. This is probably the first real Christmas she's had since she was a kid."

Hank was pleased that his friend had found a woman to love, one who would complement his life. It seemed this switch they'd decided on had been beneficial to them both, in more ways than either had anticipated. Hank walked him to the door and unlatched the lock. "I'll see you later, then."

"Later."

Hank would be joining Pete, Millie, and Gracie for Christmas dinner, too. As he recalled, Gracie was a wonderful cook. He couldn't remember the last time he'd sat down to a homemade meal of roast turkey with all the extras.

Once he finished, Hank showered and changed into jeans and a button-down shirt. He was about to drive into Kettle Springs when Walt appeared, knocking at the tavern entrance, wanting in.

"I'm closed," he told the older man as he unlocked the door.

Walt stepped inside, out of the cold. "Need a favor," he said, as he scratched the side of his beard, as if a little embarrassed.

"Sure thing." Walt was one of his best customers. In all the time he'd occupied the stool at The Last Call, the older man had never asked for anything other than a re-fill.

"Well, Rowdy and me were thinking, you know?" He hesitated, and then looked up. "Your friend Pete invited us to that church service tonight, and we were talking about some of the things he said. Before we knew Pete was a pastor, he spoke to us like we were friends."

"I believe that's the way Pete sees you, too," Hank assured him.

"The thing is, neither Rowdy nor I see that well at night any longer to drive. Short distances aren't a problem, but it's twenty miles to Bridgeport. We figured you'd be going and wondered if we could catch a ride with you."

Walt and Rowdy wanted to attend the Christmas Eve service? If they wanted to go, then he'd be willing to make it happen. "Not a problem. I'll be happy to drive you both."

"Much appreciated," Walt said, and nodded.

Would wonders never cease?

Stopping long enough to eat lunch, Hank headed into Bridgeport to see if he could lend a hand before returning to pick up Walt and Rowdy. While they were cleaning, Pete had mentioned Gracie was busy at the church, so he stopped by there first. That's where he found Gracie, Millie, and Pete hard at work. The two women were polishing the pews. The scent of pine filled the church. Pete was busy decorating the altar with sprigs of holly. Red poinsettias circled the podium, and evergreen branches were tucked on the ledge of the stained-glass windows. A decorated Christmas tree had been placed in the vestibule.

What brought a smile was the life-size manger scene, which was presumably there for the reenactment the Sunday-school children were putting on during the service. Hay was piled around the manger and a big star secured at the top of the cardboard cutout that was the stable.

Gracie was the first one to notice Hank. Her eyes revealed her surprise and then the warmth of her welcome.

"Hank," she said, setting down her rag and walking over to him.

He took her hands in his as their eyes met. He needed to kiss her, and it didn't seem right to do it inside the sanctuary. "Could you step into the vestibule for a moment?" he asked.

"Of course."

As soon as they stepped outside the main part of the church, Hank brought her into his embrace and kissed her. She all but melted in his arms. How this woman could kiss. He felt her impact from the hair at the top of his head to the bottom of his feet. He didn't think he'd ever get enough of her kisses.

When he broke off the kiss, Gracie looked up at him, blinked, and then blushed, her face turning three shades of pink. "What was that for?" she asked, clearly flustered.

"Because I can't seem to keep my hands off you. Because it's almost Christmas. Because you're the most beautiful woman I've ever known."

Her blush went from pink to red. "You're being ridiculous."

He smiled. "I suppose you're right, but that's what one should expect from a man in love."

All the color seemed to drain from her face at once. "You really love me?"

How could she doubt it? He was a fool for her, so head-over-heels in love, he couldn't think straight. "You should know you hold my heart in the palm of your hand, Grace Ann Armstrong."

For a moment it looked as if Gracie was about to cry. "I'm . . . I've been such a—"

He knew what she was about to say and stopped her by pressing his finger against her lips, cutting her off. "What you need to say now is that my feelings for you are a reflection of how strongly you feel about me." He was convinced he hadn't read her wrong. Had he? How quickly doubt filled him, tightening his chest.

"You should know better than to ask. I'm crazy about you. This is the best Christmas of my entire life."

"Mine, too." He kissed the top of her head. "Now tell me what you need me to do."

"Holding me close is what is the most appealing; however, that wouldn't be practical. The hymn books need to be straightened and placed at the proper intervals along the pews."

"You got it."

He started to drop his arms when she stopped him. "You were right, you know."

"About what?"

"About Millie. She's perfect for my brother."

Hank grinned, and then, because he couldn't stop himself, he kissed her again.

"To work," she said, but she didn't sound all that eager.

"To work," he repeated, and was unable to wipe the grin off his mouth.

That evening, Hank returned to Kettle Springs and drove both Walt and Rowdy to church with him. The two had done their best to clean up. Walt had trimmed his beard, wetted down his hair, and slicked it back with enough gel to hold up in a windstorm. He wore the same old coat, and if not for that, Hank might not have recognized the older man. Rowdy had done pretty much the same.

To be frank, Hank was a bit nervous for them as they entered the church. Even though they were early, the pews were quickly filling up. The only available room was toward the front of the church, which meant they were obliged to walk down the center aisle. Hank led the way, with Walt and Rowdy following close behind.

A buzz began as soon as they started down the long center aisle. It seemed every eye in church was on the three of them. Hank tensed, apprehensive that the two old-timers would feel uncomfortable being the center of attention.

He need not have worried. Walt removed his knit hat and held it in front of him, and after elbowing Rowdy, the other man removed his wool cap, too. As they continued toward an empty pew, Walt turned and nodded to the woman sitting at the end of a row.

"Evening," he said, and bobbed his head in greeting.

Rowdy nodded to someone on the other side.

They both continued at a slow pace, smiling and nodding at the people who lined the pews, as if they had attended this church their entire lives. It pleased him to note several "Merry Christmas" greetings followed them as they progressed toward the front.

When they approached Ken and his wife, who sat at the end of the pew, the sheriff deputy rose to his feet. He first shook Walt's hand, and then gently slapped his back before greeting Rowdy.

"Welcome, welcome," Ken greeted, as if welcoming long-lost family, and quickly introduced them to his wife and children. The three took the seats in the row in front of Ken and his wife.

By the time Pete appeared, the church was packed. Standing room only. With Gracie at the piano, the choir opened the service with two carols: "O Come, All Ye Faithful" and "Silent Night."

Walt and Rowdy belted them out at the top of their lungs, causing several people to glance their way, nod, and smile. Hank did his best not to cringe. Neither man could hold a tune, and they sang completely off-key. Hank's eye caught Gracie's as she sat at the piano and he noticed she was struggling not to laugh. It was perfect. The picture of a true Christmas.

Pete stepped up to the podium when Hank first heard the sound. At first, he was convinced he was hearing things. Yet as the sound grew closer, he knew he was right.

Motorcycles.

CHAPTER EIGHTEEN

If Pete lived to be a hundred years old, he was convinced he'd never again witness a Christmas Eve service quite like this. The singing was over, and the choir members had joined their families. Millie sat in the front pew and looked up at Pete, her warm, encouraging smile mesmerizing him. It was all he could do to tear his gaze away from her. Having her with him for this Christmas was the best gift he could ever receive.

Grace Ann moved from the piano and sat down next to Hank. Pete noticed several speculative glances when Hank slid his arm around Grace Ann's shoulders and drew her closer to his side.

It pleased him immensely that Walt and Rowdy had decided to make a showing. He hoped his talk with Walt would inspire him to reach out to his daughter one day.

The Sunday-school classes were responsible for a major part of the Christmas Eve program. The children, dressed in their costumes, sat with their families, eager to get to the part of the service where they would get to perform. Pete knew the children had been practicing for weeks for just this moment. They were ready. More than ready.

Everything was set for a lovely Christmas Eve tradition. Pete was grateful for the lessons of the last week. While filling in for Hank, he'd learned a great deal about himself and the outside world. Pete realized he'd lived a sheltered existence, surrounded by church members and other Christians. As a result, his vision had grown myopic.

Stepping around bundles of hay and the makeshift manger scene, he approached the podium. As he looked out over the congregation, one figure was decidedly missing.

Mrs. Millstone.

She normally took up an entire pew for herself, discouraging anyone from sitting next to her. The pew remained empty.

He suspected he'd seen the last of her, and while that saddened him, at the same time it was a relief. His trust was in the God he served. Briefly, he glanced toward the ceiling and the water stains that marked the area where the roof leaked, and for a short moment his faith wavered. Then he looked at Millie and his trust was restored. She did that for him. He'd given up believing he would ever find a woman who suited him. Deep down, he knew in his soul that Millie was meant to be his wife. He loved her.

He was only a minute or two into his brief message when he heard the unmistakable sound of roaring motorcycles. They seemed loud enough to break the sound barrier.

A couple short minutes later, the church doors flew open and Snake, Gunner, and the members of the Hell's Outlaws motorcycle club entered the church. People turned around to look, and a collective gasp undulated through the congregation like an ocean wave, the crest of it hitting the podium where Pete stood.

It seemed everyone in the church froze, as if not knowing what to do. Mothers placed protective arms around their children. Husbands sat up straight, as if anticipating the need to leap to their feet to protect their families.

Pete knew what he had to do. "Snake," he called out, gesturing to his muscular, tattooed friend. "Welcome to Light and Life. There's a pew right up front for you and your friends." Mrs. Millstone's space looked as if it had been reserved just for them.

Every head that had turned to stare at the back of the room swiveled toward Pete. Mouths sagged open and then closed.

"If everyone would scoot in, I believe we can make room for all our guests."

Snake and his crew, along with the ladies from Toy's, marched up the center aisle like they were part of the Macy's Thanksgiving Day parade. The strippers were dressed to the nines in knee-high cuffed black boots with three-inch heels, miniskirts, and faux-fur short jackets.

Candy paused about halfway up and smiled. Apparently recognizing a familiar face, she paused, smiled, and lifted her hand for a small wave. "Hi, Harold."

Harold's face instantly went beet red. His wife glared at him, her eyes wide with shock, before she elbowed him in the ribs. It must have hurt, because Harold jerked and pressed a hand to his side.

Snake and those with him filed into the pew, sat down as if they deserved the best seats in the house, and crossed their arms. They stared up at Pete expectantly.

Glancing at his notes, Pete decided it would be best if he went back to the beginning. Millie gave him an encouraging smile, and frankly, at that point, he needed it.

"Before I get started again, I want to welcome my friends from Kettle Springs. I'm honored that you would choose to spend Christmas Eve with us."

"Clint's madder than hops that we left him high and dry two nights running," Angel said, loud enough for the entire church to hear.

"Serves the greedy bastard right," Snake added, with a decisive nod.

The widow Laurence gasped at a swear word being spoken inside the church. She placed a hand over her heart as if she was in danger of passing out.

"We're honored you've come to join us," Pete said, wanting it understood his friends were as welcome as anyone. Language aside. He nodded at the strippers, letting them know he appreciated the sacrifice they had made.

His sermon was short and to the point, which was probably a blessing, since his friends from The Last Call were inclined to ask questions and add comments every now and again.

"How long is this supposed to take?" Gunner wanted to know.

"Shut up and let the man talk," Snake said, glaring at Gunner.

Pete continued with his sermon, going over the event of the first Christmas.

"You mean to say Mary and Joseph walked seventy-five miles from Nazareth to Bethlehem?" Kitten asked.

"Not in heels, she didn't!" Candy insisted.

"All because some hotshot wanted to count them?"

"Didn't they have census-takers back then?"

"You've got to feel for Mary. The poor woman was about to give birth."

Pete answered their questions and addressed their comments as best he could and still preach his sermon. He could see that the Sunday-school kids were getting antsy. For the younger ones, it was close to their bedtime.

"Mrs. Miller," Pete said, gesturing toward the young housewife who headed up the children's program at the church.

She rose, and the children followed her up to the front of the church. The scene was set. Mary and Joseph came center stage.

"Oh Joseph," Mary said, holding her stomach. "I believe it's time for the baby Jesus to be born." Little Mary Jane Harrison doubled over as if she was in terrible pain.

"But there's no room at the inn," Joseph told her, as if he didn't know what else to do. "I've checked everywhere."

"Try harder," Snake shouted. "Your woman needs you."

Robbie Hardy, who played the part of Joseph, looked dumbstruck, like he didn't know what to do next.

Rose Miller gestured from the sidelines for Robbie to continue.

"I'll check this one last inn," Joseph said, and walked over to a pretend door and knocked.

One of the other children made a knocking sound. The pretend door opened, and Joseph said, "My wife and I need a room. My wife is pregnant and needs to rest."

"I'm sorry. The inn is full."

Walt leaped to his feet. "For crying out loud, give the couple a room."

Robbie ignored him, and the boy playing the role of the innkeeper continued, "You can sleep in my stable for tonight. It's the best I can do."

Joseph looked out and wiped a hand across his brow as if greatly relieved. "God will bless you for this kindness," he said.

All at once, there was a loud noise that came from the back of the church and the doors flew open. With all the grandeur of a horse running in the Kentucky Derby, Hortense the mule raced down the center aisle.

The children screamed and scrambled from the front of the church. Mrs. Miller gathered them around her, like a hen protecting her brood, while Pete leaped to his feet to intercept the mule.

Only it was Gunner who grabbed hold of Hortense's reins. The mule dragged him several feet, his boots making skid marks on the church floor before he was able to stop Hortense. Then, as if this was all part of the program, Hortense bent her head and munched on the bale of hay that was part of the manger scene.

Only it wasn't just Hortense who had broken free of the barn. Two round sheep wandered in next. They paused, looked around, and then headed toward the bale of hay as if to join the mule.

"Someone left the barn door unlatched?" Willy DiGiovanni shouted the obvious. He stepped out of the pew and tried to grab one of the sheep, who made a baaing sound and scrambled away. Willy fell flat on his face in the middle of the aisle.

Someone laughed, which infuriated Willy, who was now determined to catch the sheep and return them to the barn. The sheep panicked and rushed toward Hortense. One of the men jumped onto the back of the first sheep, taking them both to the ground. Several of the men tried to help, chasing after the animals.

Pete's gaze went to Millie, who was as mesmerized as everyone else in the church. It went without saying: Bringing order back was a lost cause.

The bikers found the scene hilarious and roared with laughter. Walt slapped his thigh several times as he let loose with a loud snort.

Grace Ann buried her face in her hands, and Pete stood paralyzed, watching the crazy scene unfold before him. Some of the children were crying. Some clung to their parents. Several more were clambering toward the exit to escape before anything else could befall them.

The night was a disaster, and there wasn't much Pete could do to change it.

By the time the animals had been rounded up and returned to the barn, the church had mostly emptied. Pete couldn't blame those who chose to leave. Bikers, strippers, a runaway mule, and two sheep were enough for one night. It was an evening service few in Bridgeport were likely to forget.

Pete threw his hands into the air as he looked out over those who remained and announced, "There're cookies and hot chocolate in the church hall." He could only imagine what the good Lord would say about all this, and he believed Jesus would have a sense of humor. What else was there to do but laugh.

Finding purpose in this craziness, his sister headed toward the church hall off to the side of the sanctuary. Millie followed, he presumed to help his sister serve. Several metal buckets had been strategically placed around the area to catch the water from the leaking roof.

No one could have been more surprised than Pete when Snake and his friends followed him into the adjoining area.

"Gotta ask you, Pete, is church this much fun every week?" Snake asked, with tears of mirth in his eyes.

"No . . . tonight was an exception."

"I haven't laughed that hard in ages." He helped himself to a sugar cookie. After his first bite, his eyes brightened. "These are as good as dope. Bet they're addictive, too."

Pete grinned and reached for a cookie of his own.

Grace Ann's Christmas cookies were habit-forming, and he should know.

Walt was stuffing cookies into his coat pockets as fast as his hands could cooperate. He blushed with guilt when he noticed Pete watching him.

"Seems you're going to have plenty of these here cookies left over. Just helping you out. Be a shame for them to go to waste."

Millie handed Switchblade a cup of hot cocoa. He took a sip and then, with a horrified look, spit it out. "What the hell is this stuff?"

"Hot chocolate," Grace Ann told him.

Switchblade stared down at the cup with a huge frown. "What's in it?"

"Milk and—"

"Milk," he cried, and tossed the cup in the garbage as if it was filled with the deadliest of poisons. The hot liquid splashed against the sides of the container. "I never touch the stuff. I don't suppose you serve hot buttered rum?"

Gunner punched Switchblade's arm. "This is a church, stupid, they don't serve alcohol here."

"They should," Switchblade countered. "Bet they wouldn't have a problem filling the pews if they did."

"No doubt," Pete agreed, struggling to hide his amusement.

He approached Millie. "Quite the evening, wouldn't you say?"

"I would. The children were adorable. I feel bad they weren't able to finish the play."

"There's always next year."

Millie lowered her gaze. "Don't know that I'll be here then."

Her comment shook him. "Why wouldn't you be?"

She shrugged, as if that was answer enough.

"Don't you know how I feel about you?"

She wasn't looking at him.

"I'm not exactly like the other women in this church, Pete. I don't fit in."

"You suit me perfectly, and frankly I don't care what anyone thinks about the two of us. As far as I'm concerned, we're a couple." And, if all went as he hoped, they would one day be man and wife. Yes, it was too soon to make that kind of declaration. He accepted that things could change, although he doubted they would.

"You say that now . . ."

Pete gathered her into his arms and silenced her with a kiss. "No arguing," he said.

"But . . ."

He kissed her again. "Trust me, Millie. I know what I'm doing."

For an instant it looked as if she was about to argue. To her credit, she didn't.

Pete glanced about the room and noticed the ladies from Toy's sitting on the bikers' laps with their legs crossed and their ankles swinging. They drank the hot cocoa and sampled cookies.

Hank and Grace Ann stood side by side and seemed to have eyes only for each other.

Walt and Rowdy's cheeks looked like chipmunks' with their mouths full of nuts as they ate the cookies as fast as they could swallow.

This Christmas Eve was different from any Pete had experienced. Despite everything, he had to say it was the very best one of his life.

EPILOGUE

"That was a good story, Nana," Lily said with a big sigh, followed by a loud yawn, as she placed her hand over her mouth.

Nana looked toward the grandfather clock on the other side of the room. Pierce and Rachel would be back soon to collect the children.

"Did Hortense really bust down the church doors?" Lance asked, his tone speculative. "Or did you make that part up?"

"Every detail of that Christmas Eve service is true," Nana told him. "Hortense and the sheep, and maybe even a goat or two, although the goats arrived after the church emptied."

"Goats, too!" Lily giggled. "Did Pete end up marrying Millie?"

"He did, the following summer. They had a big wedding and nearly everyone in Bridgeport came to celebrate with them."

"What about the bikers?" Lance asked. "Did they come to the wedding?"

"Of course. Pete and the bikers were good friends. Snake was one of the groomsmen."

"Snake?" Lily's eyes widened to the size of one of Nana's snowball cookies.

Nana smiled, remembering the trouble they'd had convincing Snake to leave off his leather jacket and wear a suit. In the end, his friendship with Pete had won Snake over. He'd stood proudly next to Hank, the best man, at the altar with the two other groomsmen, Ken Lambert and Jerry White.

"What happened to Mrs. Millstone?"

Nana felt bad for the old woman. "She died the following March of a heart attack."

"It's like Hank said," Lance said. "She had heart disease."

The old woman did suffer the ailment. "She did, although when Hank mentioned her heart, he was talking about her emotional heart, not her physical one."

"What does that mean?"

"I guess the best way to explain it is to say she didn't exercise her heart enough with love. She'd rejected her only son, stewed in self-righteousness, and turned into a bitter, unhappy woman."

"Did she leave the church money so they could get a new roof?" Lance asked. He was her practical grandson.

"Sadly, no."

"Did the church ever get a new roof?"

"It did." A warmness settled over Nana at the memory. "And you'll never believe who donated the money."

Both children regarded her with open curiosity.

"The bikers. Remember when Snake, Gunner, and Switchblade attended the Christmas Eve service?"

Both children nodded.

"They saw the buckets collecting the melted snow water and decided to take care of the matter themselves. As soon as the weather permitted, they bought the roofing material and did the work themselves."

"They did?"

"Oh yes, and that's not all. They had money saved from activities that weren't helping people. After they became friends with Pete, they decided to give up doing things that might hurt others and used that money for the new roof, plus a new furnace for the church."

"They turned out to be good guys."

"They sure did," Nana agreed.

"What about Walt?" Lily asked. "Did he ever see his daughter again?"

Once more, Nana's heart warmed at the memory of the old man who had blessed them all. "It took until the following summer for Pete to convince him he would never know her reception until he tried. Walt was afraid, though."

"Why? Did he think his daughter would be angry?"

"It's hard to know. Poor Walt wrestled with what to do for months and then he had Pete make the initial contact."

"I bet Walt's daughter was happy to hear from her dad."

"She was, and Walt got to meet his grandchildren and spend time with them before he died."

"Walt died?"

"He was an old man already. He died happy, though, after seeing his daughter and holding his grandchildren."

"What about Rowdy?"

"He's gone, too. Him and Walt had hung around together for years, and Rowdy was lost without his friend. He died the following year."

Lily frowned. "I feel bad when people die."

"I know, I do, too," Nana told her sensitive granddaughter.

"What about Hank?" Lance asked. "I suppose he married Gracie."

"Oh yes, for sure."

"Does he still work at The Last Call tavern?"

"No, he sold it the following year."

"He sold the tavern?" Lance frowned and shook his head. "Bet Gracie made him do it."

"Actually, no, it was Hank's decision."

"But why? That's where all his friends were, other than Pete."

"That's the best part of the story, Lance. Hank and Snake went into business together. They own a motorcycle shop."

"Grandpa has a motorcycle shop," Lily said, bright-eyed now.

"Remember what I said when we started this story?" Nana reminded the two.

Both shook their heads.

"I said this wasn't a once-upon-a-time story. This was an in-the-beginning story."

"You mean it's true?"

"Yup. This all really happened."

"Then who's Hank?"

"He's really your grandpa Hank."

"Snake," Lance cried out. "You mean Snake is really Uncle Glen?"

Nana had a hard time hiding her smile.

"He's got a tattoo of a snake on his arm." Lance bounced against the back of the sofa as if he was in shock. "We call him Uncle Glen, even if he isn't actually our uncle. What happened to the rest of the bikers?"

"Gunner worked at the motorcycle shop for about ten years and then moved to Seattle. Switchblade joined another club and we heard from him now and again through the years. Both married and had children."

"Uncle Glen has grandkids now, too."

"He sure does."

"Did he marry Kitten?"

"No, he married one of the ladies he met in church. It was love at first sight for him and Melody. It was after he met her that he approached your grandpa about them getting a Harley-Davidson franchise together."

"He fell for a woman?" Lance shook his head in disgust.

"You love your aunt Melody," Nana reminded him.

"Whatever happened to Kitten, Candy, and Angel?" Lily wanted to know.

"I'm glad you asked." For her part, this was the best part of the story. "The Ladies Missionary Society were true to their word. They befriended the girls and went to see them once a week for a long time. On Valentine's Day, the ladies had a luncheon in their honor and had a woman tell them about other job openings in the area if they were interested. For the first time, they were given the opportunity to work elsewhere. Several of the ladies took advantage and applied for other jobs."

"If Clint was mad before, I bet he was really mad after that."

"He was, but that's a different story."

"Will you tell us that story one day?" Lance asked.

"Perhaps when you're older." It wasn't one Nana would relish telling, as Clint was responsible for the fire that burned part of the church sanctuary. It helped that insurance had covered the damage, and Clint ended up going to prison for arson.

"Nana? If Grandpa is Hank, then that means you're Gracie." Lily twisted her head to stare at her nana as if seeing her for the first time.

"That's right."

"And you're my mommy's mommy."

"Right again."

"That is so cool."

Nana smiled.

"You forgot Pete," Lance reminded her.

"Do you think I would forget my own brother?" Nana teased.

"Uncle Pete lives in Spokane now," Lily said, pressing her finger to her lip as she took all this information in. "Aunt Millie lives with him, and Uncle Pete pastors a church there."

"That's right." Nana was proud of her brother. Pete and Millie had four children, and Pete taught theology at a local private college. Millie was busy with volunteer work with the homeless and those struggling to make a better life for themselves.

"And Phillip and Luke, Ruth and Eva are our cousins."

"Right again."

"Is this story why Christmas is your favorite time of year, Nana?"

"Of course. That's when I fell in love with your grandpa."

A voice rang out from the kitchen as Rachel came to collect the children.

"Mommy, Mommy," Lily said, flying off the sofa like a jet off an aircraft carrier. "Nana told us the best story ever."

Rachel lifted her daughter into her arms. "What did she tell you?"

"It was about her and Grandpa. Did you know he used to own a tavern and Uncle Glen was part of a motorcycle club?"

"I did."

"She's Nana and Grandpa's daughter, so of course she'd know," Lance grumbled.

"It was the best story ever," Lily insisted.

"What did you think?" Rachel asked her son.

He shrugged. "It was good except for the romantic parts."

"Lance covered his ears," Lily said, tattling on her brother.

Rachel laughed. "Come on, you two, your dad's waiting in the car. Collect your coats and mittens and let's head home. It's past your bedtime already."

Rachel set Lily back down, and both children raced to collect their belongings.

"Thanks again, Mom," Rachel said.

"It's always a joy." She walked them to the door and saw them off, waving as the family drove off into the night.

No sooner had they left when Hank appeared. He wrapped his arms around her and kissed her.

"How'd it go with the little ones?" he asked. "Did you tell them another story?"

"You know how they love my stories. I told them about the Christmas before we married."

Hank tossed back his head and laughed. "That Christmas Eve is one I'll never forget. Bet the grands loved hearing about it."

"They did."

"Loved you then and love you even more now," her husband said. "Nothing's changed in all these years."

That was their first Christmas together, she recalled, and every year since then had been better, richer, and full of love.

Available in one volume for the first time:
That Wintry Feeling and *Thanksgiving Prayer*,
two of Debbie Macomber's classic novels
that explore the power of faith and the hope
of the holiday season.

The Perfect Holiday

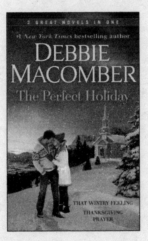

Read on for a special sneak peek!

Available soon from Ballantine Books

That Wintry Feeling

CHAPTER ONE

Cathy Thompson's long nails beat an impatient tempo against the Formica countertop as she waited.

"Yes, I'll hold," she said, and breathed heavily into the telephone. Her deep gray eyes clashed with Linda Ericson's, who sat at the table, a large newspaper spread over the top.

"Any luck?" Linda whispered.

A voice at the other end of the line interrupted Cathy's response, and she straightened, her fingers tightening around the phone. "This is Cathy Thompson again." The inflection of her voice conveyed the irritation. "Would it be possible to speak to Grady Jones?"

"Grady's in the air," a gruff male voice informed her. "Be with you in a minute, Harry," he said to someone who was obviously waiting in his office.

"When do you expect him back?" Cathy asked in her most businesslike voice.

A lengthy pause followed, and Cathy could hear the rustle of paper in the background. "Thursday afternoon. Will you hold the line a minute?"

Cathy's sigh was full of exasperation. Cradling the telephone against her shoulder with the side of her head, she pulled out a piece of paper and a pencil. As she looked up she happened to catch a glimpse of the school play yard. The sights and sounds of the last recess of the day drifted in through the open window. Her gray eyes softened as she unconsciously sought Angela Jones. A frown creased her narrow forehead as she discovered the pigtailed first-grader leaning against the play shed, watching the other girls jump rope. Angela always seemed to be on the outside looking in.

"Do you want to leave a message?" The harried male voice came back on the phone.

"I've already left four," Cathy snapped.

"Listen, all I do is take the message. If Grady doesn't return your call, it's not my fault." He hesitated. "Are you the gal from the school again?"

"Yes, I'm the gal from the school again." She echoed his words, doing her best to disguise her frustration.

"All I can tell you is that Grady is flying on assignment. I'll tell him you phoned."

The man wasn't to blame if Grady Jones didn't wish to speak to her, and Cathy's reply was less agitated. "Please do that." Gently, she replaced the receiver in its cradle.

"Well?" Linda looked up expectantly.

"No luck. It's the same as before. They'll take a message, but he won't be back until Thursday afternoon."

"What are you going to do?" Linda asked, concern knitting her brow.

Cathy shrugged. "Maybe it's time I personally introduced myself to the elusive Grady Jones. He'll have a hard time not talking to me if I show up at the airfield." Cathy had done her research well. The school information card had been sketchy. The card listed the father's occupation as pilot, employed by Alaska Cargo Company. No business phone number had been given, and when Cathy looked it up in the yellow pages she found a large commercial ad. The fine print at the bottom of the advertisement stated that Grady Jones was the company owner. The information card had stated that Angela had no mother. Cathy had found the comment an interesting one. How could any child not have a mother? It could be that Angela's parents were divorced. What Cathy couldn't understand was how someone as unconcerned and uncaring as Grady Jones could have been awarded custody of the child. Cathy had tried on several occasions to contact him at home, but the only adult she had ever reached was a housekeeper, who promised to give him a message. Cathy had stopped counting the times she'd left messages for him.

"After all the trouble you've gone through, I'd say that's about the only way you're going to get his attention."

"Believe me, I won't have any problem getting his attention. His ears will burn for a week."

"Cathy . . ." Linda warned, her large brown eyes worried. "Alienating Angela's father won't help her."

"I know, but I can't help but dislike the man."

The bell rang, indicating the end of recess. Emitting a soft groan, Cathy turned around. "Back to the salt mine." It had been another break wasted trying to contact a parent. Next time she'd pour herself a cup of coffee before making a phone call.

"Don't go yet," Linda called. "I want to read you this personal."

"Linda," Cathy said with a sigh, but she knew better than to argue. Her friend would insist that she listen anyway. "All right, but be quick about it."

Rustling the paper, Linda sat upright and read. "Sincere gentleman seeking sincere lady for sincere relationship—"

"Only sincere women need apply," Cathy interrupted. "Dull, Linda, dull. If you insist on playing matchmaker, the least you can do is find someone with a little personality."

"Okay, here's another." She glanced up. "Man with large house, large cat, six kids. Cat not enough."

"Six kids." Cathy choked.

"That says a lot," Linda defended. "At least he's honest and forthright. He must like animals."

"That would make Peterkins happy, but unfortunately I'm the one that has to be satisfied. Six kids are out."

The shuffle of feet could be heard above the laughter as the children filed into the school building. The afternoon could no longer be delayed.

Two hours later, Cathy was about to unlock the door to her rental house on Lacey Street. She had rented a home so that Peterkins, her black cocker spaniel, would have a yard in which to roam. Steve had given her Peterkins, and the dog was probably the only good thing she had left of their relationship. In the beginning she had resented the fact that Peterkins had been a gift from Steve. Every time she looked at her floppy-eared friend she was reminded of a soured relationship. But Peterkins wasn't to be blamed, and there was far more than a dog to remind her of Steve. It was funny how many of her thoughts he continued to dominate. Yet it was totally, completely over. Steve was a married man. A knot twisted the sensitive muscles of her stomach. He'd been married for five months and six days. Not that she was counting. Bravely, she had attended the wedding, had been a member of the wedding party. The maid of honor. Her sister wouldn't hear of anything else.

Exhaling a quivering breath, Cathy turned the key in the lock and pushed open the door. Immediately Peterkins was there, excitedly jumping up and down. When she crouched down to pet him, he fervently lapped her hand with his moist tongue.

"Let me relax a minute, and we'll go for our walk," Cathy told him. Peterkins knew her moods better than anyone, Cathy mused while she changed clothes and sorted through the mail. Peeling an orange, she sat at the small circular table in her kitchen and leaned against the back of the chair.

Memories of Steve again ruled her thoughts. They'd quarreled. It wasn't any major disagreement; she couldn't even recall what it was that had sparked the argument. But something was different this time. Cathy had decided she was tired of always being the one to give in, apologize, change. They had talked about getting married on several occasions. If their relationship was to be a lasting one, Cathy had decided, then Steve must learn to do his share of giving. It would be a good lesson for him to admit he was wrong for once.

She pulled each of the orange segments apart and set them on the napkin, fingering each one. Her appetite was gone, and she scooted the afternoon snack away.

The whole idea of teaching Steve a lesson had been immature and foolish. Cathy realized that now. She gave a short laugh. What a wonderful thing hindsight was.

When Steve began dating her sister, MaryAnne, Cathy had been amused. He wasn't fooling her; she knew exactly what he was doing. She had taken great pride in meeting him at the door when he came to pick up Mary-Anne for a date. With a cheery smile, she had proven she wasn't in the least bit jealous. He could date whom he liked. Twice she had arranged dates at the same time MaryAnne and Steve would be going out so that they would all meet at the apartment she shared with her sister.

The only one who had shown any concern over such foolishness had been their mother.

"Mom." Cathy had strived to brush off Paula Thompson's concern. "MaryAnne and I cut the apron strings when we moved out and got an apartment of our own. From now on you're only supposed to give advice when we ask. Remember?" Her words were a teasing reminder of what their mother had told them when they decided to move in together. Although her mother never mentioned a word again about MaryAnne and Steve, the question was in her eyes.

Six weeks had passed, and still Steve continued to play his game in an attempt to make her jealous. If she hadn't been so stubborn she would have seen what was happening. Twice MaryAnne had come to her.

"You don't mind, do you?" The gray eyes so like her own had pleaded. "I'd stop seeing him in a minute if our relationship was hurting you in any way."

Cathy had laughed lightly. "It's over," she said with a flippant air. "It was over a long time ago. There's no need to concern yourself."

Then one night MaryAnne had burst into the apartment and proudly displayed the beautiful diamond engagement ring. Cathy had been shocked. This was carrying things to an extreme. Steve had gone too far. She wasn't going to allow him to use her little sister like this for another minute.

The argument when she'd confronted Steve had been loud and bitter. They'd hurled accusations at each other faster and sharper than a machine gun.

All through the preparations for the wedding Cathy had expected Steve to put a halt to things. It was unbelievable that a minor disagreement three months before had been allowed to go this far.

Throughout the time they had prepared for the wedding, MaryAnne had been radiantly happy. A hundred times Cathy had to bite her tongue to keep from saying. "Listen, Sis, I'm not completely sure Steve loves you. He loves me, I know he does." Maybe she should have said it.

The message was in her eyes; her mother read it the morning of the wedding. Steve saw it as she marched up the aisle preceding her sister. It was there when the minister pronounced Steve and MaryAnne man and wife.

The memory of those words seemed to echo, assaulting her from all sides. Urgently, Cathy stood and pushed her chair to the table. She needed to get out, away from the memories, the hurt.

"Bring me the leash, Peterkins," she said to her dog, who promptly stepped into the bedroom and pulled the rhinestone-studded strap off the chair. Cathy paused, fingering the red leather. The leash had been another gift from Steve. Would he continue to haunt her for the rest of her life? Would it always be like this?

For two months after the wedding Cathy had walked around in a haze of pain and disillusionment. This couldn't be happening to her. This wasn't real. It became almost impossible to hide her emotions from her family. She had to get away, to the ends of the earth. Alaska. The opportunity to work as a basic skills instructor had come as a surprise. Her application had been submitted months before. She had never intended to accept the job, even if it was offered to her. She had done it to tease Steve, telling him if he didn't proclaim his undying love she'd abandon him for parts unknown. Willingly, Steve had obliged. When she hadn't heard from the school district, Cathy was relieved. It had been a fluke, a joke. Now it was her salvation, a lifeline to sanity.

No one had understood her reasons for going—except her mother, and perhaps Steve. With a sense of urgency she had gone about building a new life for herself. Forming friendships, reaching out. It was only in the area of men that she withdrew, held back. Eventually that reserve would abate. A soft smile curved up the edges of her lips. Linda and those crazy personal ads she was always reading to her. If her friend had anything to do with it, Cathy would be married by Christmas.

Thanksgiving Prayer

CHAPTER ONE

The radiant blue heavens drew Claudia Masters's eyes as she boarded the jet for Nome, Alaska. Her heart rate accelerated with excitement. In less than two hours she would be with Seth—manly, self-assured, masterful Seth. She made herself comfortable and secured the seat belt, anticipating the rumble of the engines that would thrust the plane into the air.

She had felt some uncertainty when she boarded the plane that morning in Seattle. But she'd hastily placed a phone call during her layover in Anchorage and been assured by Seth's assistant that yes, he had received her message, and yes, he would meet her at the airport. Confident now, Claudia relaxed and idly flipped through a magazine.

A warmth, a feeling of contentment, filled her. Cooper's doubts and last-ditch effort to change her mind were behind her now, and she was free to make her life with Seth.

Cooper had been furious with her decision to leave medical school. But he was only her uncle. He hadn't understood her love for her Alaskan oilman, just as he couldn't understand her faith in the Lord.

A smile briefly curved her soft mouth upward. Cooper had shown more emotion in that brief twenty-minute visit to his office than she'd seen in all her twenty-five years.

"Quitting med school is the dumbest idea I've ever heard," he'd growled, his keen brown eyes challenging the serene blue of hers.

"Sometimes loving someone calls for unusual behavior," she had countered, knowing anything impractical was foreign to her uncle.

For a moment all Cooper could do was stare at her. She could sense the anger drain from him as he lowered himself into the desk chair.

"Contrary to what you may believe, I have your best interests at heart. I see you throwing away years of study for some ignorant lumberjack. Can you blame me for doubting your sanity?"

"Seth's an oilman, not a lumberjack. There aren't any

native trees in Nome." It was easier to correct Cooper than to answer the questions that had plagued her, filling her with doubts. The choice hadn't been easy; indecision had tormented her for months. Now that she'd decided to marry Seth and share his life in the Alaskan wilderness, a sense of joy and release had come over her.

"It's taken me two miserable months to realize that my future isn't in any hospital," she continued. "I'd be a rotten doctor if I couldn't be a woman first. I love Seth. Someday I'll finish medical school, but if a decision has to be made, I'll choose Seth Lessinger every time."

But Cooper had never been easily won over. The tense atmosphere became suddenly quiet as he digested the thought. He expelled his breath, but it was several seconds before he spoke. "I'm not thinking of myself, Claudia. I want you to be absolutely sure you know what you're doing."

"I am," she replied with complete confidence.

Now, flying high above the lonely, barren Alaska tundra, Claudia continued to be confident she was doing the right thing. God had confirmed the decision. Seth had known from the beginning, but it had taken her much longer to realize the truth.

Gazing out the plane window, she viewed miles upon miles of the frozen, snow-covered ground. It was just as Seth had described: a treeless plain of crystalline purity.

There would be a summer, he'd promised, days that ran into each other when the sun never set. Flowers would blossom, and for a short time the tundra would explode into a grassy pasture. Seth had explained many things about life in the North. At first she'd resented his letters, full of enticements to lure her to Nome. If he really loved her, she felt, he should be willing to relocate in Seattle until she'd completed her studies. It wasn't so much to ask. But as she came to know and love Seth, it became evident that Nome was more than the location of his business. It was a way of life, Seth's life. Crowded cities, traffic jams, and shopping malls would suffocate him.

She should have known that the minute she pushed the cleaning cart into the motel room. Her being a housekeeper at the Wilderness Motel had been something of a miracle in itself.

Leaning back, Claudia slowly lowered her lashes as the memories washed over her.

Ashley Robbins, her lifetime friend and roommate, had been ill—far too sick to spend the day cleaning rooms. By the time Ashley admitted as much, it was too late to call the motel and tell them she wouldn't be coming to work, so Claudia had volunteered to go in her place.

Claudia had known from the moment she slid the pass

key into the lock that there was something different, something special, about this room.

Her hands rested on her slender hips as she looked around. A single man slept here. She smiled as she realized how accurate she was becoming at describing the occupants of each room, and after just one day. She was having fun speculating. Whoever was staying in here had slept uneasily. The sheet and blankets were pulled free of the mattress and rumpled haphazardly at the foot of the king-size bed.

As she put on the clean sheets, she couldn't help wondering what Cooper would think if he could see her now. He would be aghast to know she was doing what he would call "menial work."

As she lifted the corner of the mattress to tuck in the blanket, she noticed an open Bible on the nightstand, followed by the sudden feeling that she wasn't alone. As she turned around, a smile lit up her sky-blue eyes. But her welcome died: no one was there.

After finishing the bed, she plugged in the vacuum. With the flip of the switch the motor roared to life. A minute later she had that same sensation of being watched, and she turned off the machine. But when she turned, she once again discovered she was alone.

Pausing, she studied the room. There was something about this place: not the room itself, but the occupant.

She could sense it, feel it: a sadness that seemed to reach out and touch her, wrapping itself around her. She wondered why she was receiving these strange sensations. Nothing like this had ever happened to her before.

A prayer came to her lips as she silently petitioned God on behalf of whoever occupied this room. When she finished she released a soft sigh. Once, a long time ago, she remembered reading that no one could come to the Lord unless someone prayed for them first. She wasn't sure how scriptural that was, but the thought had stuck with her. Often she found herself offering silent prayers for virtual strangers.

After cleaning the bathroom and placing fresh towels on the rack, she began to wheel the cleaning cart into the hallway. Again she paused, brushing wisps of copper-colored hair from her forehead as she examined the room. She hadn't forgotten anything, had she? Everything looked right. But again that terrible sadness seemed to reach out to her.

Leaving the cart, she moved to the desk and took out a postcard and a pen from the drawer. In large, bold letters she printed one of her favorite verses from Psalms. It read: "May the Lord give you the desire of your heart and make all your plans succeed." Psalm 20:4. She didn't question why that particular verse had come to mind. It didn't offer solace, even though she had felt unhappiness here. Perplexed and a little unsure, she tucked the card into the corner of the dresser mirror.

Back in the hall, she checked to be sure the door had locked automatically. Her back ached. Ashley hadn't been kidding when she said this was hard work. It was that and more. She was so glad that had been her final room for the day. A thin sheen of perspiration covered Claudia's brow, and she pushed her thick, naturally curly hair from her face. Her attention was still focused on the door when she began wheeling the cart toward the elevator. She hadn't gone more than a few feet when she struck something. A quick glance upward told her that she'd run into a man.

"I'm so sorry," she apologized immediately. "I wasn't watching where I was going." Her first impression was that this was the largest, most imposing man she'd ever seen. He loomed above her, easily a foot taller than her five-foot-five frame. His shoulders were wide, his waist and hips lean, and he was so muscular that the material of his shirt was pulled taut across his broad chest. He was handsome in a reckless-looking way, his hair magnificently dark. His well-trimmed beard was a shade lighter.

"No problem." The stranger smiled, his mouth sensuous and appealing, his eyes warm.

Claudia liked that. He might be big, but one look told her he was a gentle giant.

Not until she was in her car did she realize she hadn't watched to see if the giant had entered the room where she'd gotten such a strange feeling.

By the time Claudia got back to the apartment, Ashley looked better. She was propped against the arm of the sofa, her back cushioned by several pillows. A hand-knit afghan covered her, and a box of tissues sat on the coffee table, the crumpled ones littering the polished surface.

"How'd it go?" she asked, her voice scratchy and unnatural. "Were you able to figure out one end of the vacuum from the other?"

"Of course." Claudia laughed. "I had fun playing house, but next time warn me—I broke my longest nail."

"That's the price you pay for being so stubborn," Ashley scolded as she grabbed a tissue, anticipating a sneeze. "I told you it was a crazy idea. Did old Burns say anything?"

"No, she was too grateful. Finding a replacement this late in the day would have been difficult."

Fall classes at the University of Washington had resumed that Monday, and Ashley had been working at the motel for only a couple of weeks, one of the two part-time jobs she had taken to earn enough to stay in school.

Claudia knew Ashley had been worried about losing the job, so she'd been happy to step in and help. Her own tuition and expenses were paid by a trust fund her father had established before his death. She had offered to lend Ashley money on numerous occasions, but her friend had stubbornly refused. Ashley believed that if God wanted her to have a degree in education, then He would provide the necessary money. Apparently He did want that for her, because the funds were always there when she needed them.

Ashley's unshakable faith had taught Claudia valuable lessons. She had been blessed with material wealth, while Ashley struggled from one month to the next. But of the two of them, Claudia considered Ashley the richer.

Claudia often marveled at her friend's faith. Everything had been taken care of in her own life. Decisions had been made for her. As for her career, she'd known from the time she was in grade school that she would be a doctor, a dream shared by her father. The last Christmas before his death he'd given her a stethoscope. Later she realized that he must have known he wouldn't be alive to see their dream fulfilled. Now there was only Cooper, her pompous, dignified uncle.

"How are you feeling?"

Ashley sneezed into a tissue, which did little to muffle the sound. "Better," she murmured, her eyes red and watery. "I should be fine by tomorrow. I don't want you to have to fill in for me again."

"We'll see," Claudia said, hands on her hips. Ashley

was so stubborn, she mused—she seemed to be surrounded by strong-willed people.

Later that night she lay in bed, unable to sleep. She hadn't told Ashley about what had happened in the last room she'd cleaned. She didn't know how she could explain it to anyone. Now she wished she'd waited to see if the stranger outside had been the one occupying that room. The day had been unusual in more ways than one. With a yawn, she rolled over and forced herself to relax and go to sleep.